CHAPTER I
A VOICE IN THE SKY

The sun had sunk behind the mountains some time ago, but an afterglow lit the western sky like a furnace. It seemed almost as if the distant Imperial Isle was on fire.

Quinn turned away from the sight and looked to the east. The coming night was spreading its wings above scant pine trees and shadowed mountaintops. In less than an hour it would be fully dark.

A rising wind, stronger than the last, ruffled his hair and stung his eyes. He shivered at its deep, cold bite and drew his cloak closer around him.

1

Winter had come sooner than expected. Out here on the exposed mountainside, they were at the weather's mercy. At least Ignus and Ulric had helped to get a campfire started before they set off scouting. That had been hours ago.

'Remind me again why we're up here instead of in a warm inn?' Thea grumbled. She huddled closer to the flames, her long red hair almost catching in them.

'Because of the amazing view,' Quinn joked, sitting down beside her. Seeing her scowl, he added, 'And because we're staying out of the way of Black Guard patrols.'

'What patrols? I haven't seen a single Black Guard since we got to this island!'

'Hmm,' Quinn murmured. Thea was right; it had been suspiciously quiet lately on the Black Guard front. 'Perhaps they're all tucked up cosily in their barracks, eating and drinking their way through our taxes.'

'Wishing you were still with them?' Thea asked, with a half-smile.

'Gods, no!'

The wind rose again, bringing a few dancing snowflakes with it. Quinn sucked air sharply through his teeth. 'Whoever called this island the "Golden Sun" must have been off his head on fermented wartberries. It's freezing!'

'I think you'll find that *was* the gods, Quinn. "A golden sun they set to the East of the Imperial Isle, and a silver moon to the West, that men might know their handiwork." *Book of Makings*, chapter one, verse six.'

'Never had you down for a religious type.'

Thea shrugged. 'I'm not. But it makes for a nice story.'

'Speaking of books, how are you getting on with the one Mrs Onyx gave you?'

Thea brightened at once. She drew the slim black spell book from the folds of her clothes and held it open on her lap.

'It's great! I've already mastered three of the major glyphs, and I'm nearly there with the Sassenava Incantation. Although there's one tricky bit where you have to sort of *hiccup*, because it's written in the Lost Speech of Eld and that's how you pronounce . . .' Her voice trailed off as Quinn held up a hand.

'Short version?' he asked.

'I can do more stuff.' Thea grinned wolfishly. 'How about you? How's the dragonblood that's pumping through your veins?'

Quinn looked at the outline of his hand, where the light of the fire shining through made his skin glow blood-red. *Dragonblood*, he thought. It hardly seemed real.

In the last few weeks he'd learnt things about himself that he could never have imagined. To start with he had dragonblood – the ability to shift his form into that of a dragon. And as if that wasn't enough, his dragonblood was royal. Quinn was the lost son of the Emperor and Empress.

His father, Emperor Marek, had been an Earth-type dragonblood, giving him power over stones, minerals and metal. Quinn was sure he'd inherited that same power, and the way he'd melted a fearsome stone troll into slurry seemed to confirm it. He was capable of even more, he knew that. So far, though, he'd hardly had time to scratch the surface of his new powers.

'We should practise,' Quinn said. 'It'll kill some time while we wait for Ignus and Ulric.'

Thea glanced up at the thickening snowfall. 'Good idea. Maybe it'll take my mind off this filthy weather, too.'

Quinn rubbed his hands together until they tingled. Nearby lay a boulder about the size of his head. He took a breath and began to concentrate.

'What are you doing?' Thea asked.

'Melting it!'

'What for?'

'Just watch,' Quinn muttered through gritted teeth.

He felt power radiate from him, building between his hands and lashing out into the rock.

Change, he willed it. *Shift your form . . .*

Thea looked on, the flames lighting up her freckles, as the rock warped and flexed before them. It was solid granite, but Quinn moulded it with his mind as if it were soft clay. He stretched two crude wings out of it, made a head bulge from the front and tweaked a beak into place, then added two stubby little legs.

'It's a bird!' Thea laughed.

Quinn wiped sweat from his forehead. 'There. Not bad for a first try, huh?'

'Not bad at all. Now it's my turn. Let's see . . .' Thea leafed through her spell book until she found a page filled with runes like thorns and claws. She held the book open with one hand and gestured with the other. '*Verem, vita, aeolus!*'

The stone bird twitched. Its beak snapped. It gave a single hoarse croak and beat its wings as if it was trying to fly.

Thea wrinkled her nose, unsatisfied, and muttered something. Silently, the bird floated up into the air. Her finger moved with it, as if joined by an invisible string.

Quinn clapped. 'Come on, little guy! You can do it!'

'I'm giving him some help,' Thea laughed. She raised her arm and the bird, still flapping awkwardly, rose into the snowy night sky above them.

Without warning, the sky lit up. A curtain of seething blue light tore across their view from one end to the other. The clouds overhead shrank back.

Quinn jumped to his feet. Thea gasped. Her concentration broke. The stone bird, suddenly motionless, fell like a brick to shatter on a rock below.

'What *is* that?' Quinn said.

'The Seraphic Lights!' Thea breathed. 'Of course . . . This high in the mountains, you can see them clearly.'

Quinn looked in amazement at the rippling light show before them. He wasn't sure if it was magical, or natural, or some weird combination of both. There was beauty in the uncanny light, but Quinn felt dread stealing up inside him. Something evil was at hand. He could feel it in the air.

'Look!' His hand shot out, pointing to where ragged dark holes were appearing in the misty light. No, not holes – *eyes*. Then a cruel slash of a mouth opened below. The image of a terrible face formed before them, hundreds of feet tall. A face he knew.

Quinn bared his teeth as a surge of hatred hit him. 'Vayn!'

The gigantic face laughed, and the laughter thundered down the mountainside, shaking the powdery snow loose. Quinn stood his ground, glaring back at the image of the Emperor: the usurper, the tyrant and the man who'd murdered his parents.

'Little children, you are very far from home,' Vayn gloated. 'Do you think that your pitiful rebellion has a chance, now that you have released both Ulric and Ignus? Bravo. Two mighty Dragon Knights . . . a dullard and a rogue!'

Quinn drew a breath to shout defiance in Vayn's face, but Thea gripped his arm. 'Don't make a sound,' she hissed in his ear. 'You'll bring down an avalanche on top of us.'

Vayn's features twisted, no longer mocking but a demonic mask of fury. His voice rose to a shriek as he spoke. 'Heed me now. Crawl back to where you came from, little worm, and hide. Persist, and I warn you, my agents are everywhere. I will find you, and when I do, I will hang your ragged corpse from the palace walls as a warning to all other dragonblood filth!'

The deformed curtain of light suddenly collapsed and flickered out, as if Vayn's rage was too much for it to bear. The menacing face of Alariss's ruler was gone.

Quinn and Thea stood, breathing hard, looking at one another.

'Just so you know,' said Thea with a nervous laugh, 'we're not going to take the "run-away-and-hide" option, right?'

'You can if you like,' Quinn said. 'I'm going to free the rest of the Dragon Knights. And we're taking Vayn down.' He grabbed another lump of wood and threw it into the fire, hard. A shower of sparks went up. 'If that little show was meant to scare me, it didn't work.'

Thea gave him a doubtful look, but kept her mouth shut.

Quinn stared into the fire and thought about how far he'd already come. Only a few weeks ago he and his Aunt Marta had been living on the backwater island of Yaross, where nothing important ever happened. Then one day Vayn's Black Guard had come calling, looking for new recruits. Together he and Thea, a fellow trainee, had escaped and had found out the truth about Quinn's real parentage.

The official story Vayn had spread told of how the Dragon Knights had betrayed and murdered the Imperial Family. Quinn knew that was a lie now. The loyal Dragon Knights had been exiled, forced to wear magical manacles that robbed them of their shape-shifting powers.

Guided by his enchanted golden sword, an heirloom from his royal father, Quinn and Thea had set out to free the six Dragon Knights and unite the islands of Alariss in rebellion. So far, Ignus the Flame Dragon and Ulric the Shadow Dragon had joined them, and the whispers of revolution were starting to grow. But there was still a long, perilous road left to travel.

'They're back!' Thea yelled.

Two dragons swooped silently out of the sky and landed on the mountain path. Quinn ran to meet them. 'Ignus! Ulric! What took you so long?'

'We had to be sure! The Island of the Golden Sun is riddled with mountain passes and narrow trails,' rumbled Ignus.

'Perfect places for an ambush,' Ulric added. 'But the only Black Guards we could see are camped in the valleys.'

'So what are we waiting for? We're here for Nord the Storm Dragon, right? And the sword showed us he was close. Let's go and get him!'

Fire flashed in Ignus's eyes for a moment. 'Yes, he is close. It seems he is in his ancestral home, the Auric Citadel, which sits like an eagle's nest on top of the highest, bleakest mountain on this island.'

'We'll have to fly,' Ulric explained.

Quinn shrugged. 'No problem.' He focused his will, listening to the throb of dragonblood in his veins, and forced himself to change.

A violent shudder ripped through his body and flung him onto his hands and knees. His skin mottled, warped and became golden scales that glistened in the firelight. Bones cracked as his neck stretched and his jaw elongated. A moment's straining, and with a sound like unfurling sails, two vast wings exploded from his back.

In seconds, Quinn had become a golden dragon. His huge chest heaved like a bellows. *I'm getting the hang of this,* he thought.

Thea sniffed at him. 'Show-off,' she muttered. But she climbed onto his back anyway.

Beating their wings until a whirl of snowflakes danced around them, the three dragons and Thea launched themselves into the air . . .

CHAPTER 2

A FROSTY WELCOME

In dragonform, Quinn couldn't even feel the cold. He relished the rush of air across his wings and the thrill of brushing up against the clouds, which felt like a thin, damp mist. To fly as a dragon was to be free.

The temptation to swoop, dive and loop-the-loop up here in the icy air was almost overpowering, but he knew Thea wouldn't appreciate stunt flying. Instead, he nestled into the slipstream behind Ignus and Ulric.

The two Dragon Knights winged ahead like vast ornamental kites, beating their wings only occasionally to gain height and then gliding swiftly through the air. Quinn understood why. This cross-country journey was a stealth flight. The sound of wing beats might alert any Black Guards who were stationed down below.

The mountainous landscape rolled past beneath him, a world in miniature. Bare hills and crags looked like uneven plaster; forests were like clutches of moss on a rock wall. The clouds and snow were clearing now and the moon was almost full.

Up ahead, the shape of a single huge mountain loomed, dominating the landscape. They approached silently, coming closer and closer, until the sheer rock wall seemed to fill Quinn's view.

Then, abruptly, Ignus and Ulric beat their wings hard and went into a steep ascent, racing upwards only a few dozen feet away from the rock face. Quinn followed, changing course just in time.

'Hey!' Thea yelped as she was flung backwards. Quinn couldn't even feel her nails digging into his scales as she clung on.

Like rockets they swept up into the air, not stopping until they were high above the mountain's peak. Quinn looked down and saw an incredible sight below him.

In the moonlight, the Auric Citadel stood revealed on the mountaintop, a delicate-looking fantasy of pale stone towers and domed golden roofs. It seemed not to have been built on the mountain so much as carved out of it, as if some skilled craftsman had scraped away the upper stone of the rocky peak to reveal towers, plunging walls, turrets, battlements, bridges and walkways. Quinn couldn't decide if it was a castle the size of a city, or a city so fortified it looked like a castle.

The dragons circled, looking for a landing spot.

Quinn took in the Citadel. It was shaped like a crown on a domed head; towers circled around an outer wall, and a slender white tower rose from the very centre.

All over the dome, steep mountain paths and smart-looking streets connected the squares, balconies and plateaus. Lines of street lamps glittered blue like strings of diamonds; thousands of windows shone from the walls like a dusting of gold.

'Ready, Ulric?' rumbled Ignus.

'Ready!'

Before Quinn could ask what was going on, both dragons shimmered and changed before him. Suddenly, he was flying alongside two eagles and his own wings looked feathery instead of scaled. *Of course*, he thought. They could hardly fly down into the city in dragonform without being noticed. Ulric must be disguising them.

'A little warning, maybe?' Thea gasped, clutching feathers where once there'd been scales.

'Tell that to Ulric!' Quinn called.

Next moment, they dived down towards the Citadel.

Quinn folded his wings and shot down with them, hoping he could slow down in time. Thea let out a low moan – whether from fear or airsickness, he couldn't tell.

The group landed just inside the Citadel's outer wall, on the roof of what seemed to be some sort of grain storehouse. There was nobody at all in sight, and no lamps burned nearby.

The air flickered and Ulric and Ignus were dragons again, then humans. Quinn shifted back into human form himself, with Thea hastily hopping off his back.

'You're a little out of practice, old friend,' Ignus told Ulric, patting him on the shoulder. 'The whole point of making us look like eagles was so we wouldn't attract attention.'

Ulric shrugged. 'And?'

'You forgot Quinn had a passenger. Riding an eagle is about as conspicuous as riding a dragon, you know.'

'What choice did I have?' Ulric said, chuckling. 'And besides, it was kind of funny . . .'

Quinn didn't seem impressed. He walked to the battlements at the building's edge and looked out over the Citadel. 'This place is like some kind of labyrinth,' he said. 'It's probably crawling with Black Guards.'

'Not likely,' said Ulric. 'I doubt there's a single Black Guard here.'

Quinn turned around and gaped at him. 'But Vayn himself said he had agents everywhere . . .'

'Vayn's arm reaches far, but not as far as the Auric Citadel, Quinn,' Ignus interrupted. 'This place is fortified by a power older than either magic or dragonblood: *gold*. The Citadel is literally sitting on a goldmine. There are tunnels down into this mountain that run for miles.'

'The Seven Families are rich,' put in Ulric. 'Stinking-to-high-heaven rich.'

Seven towers, seven families, thought Quinn. *All wealthy from the gold they've mined and hoarded. So the island of the Golden Sun is golden after all . . .*

'How can you protect a city with gold?' Thea asked, puzzled.

'You hire the best mercenaries money can buy to be your family's own private army,' said Ulric. 'The Seven Families want to be left alone with their gold, and Vayn knows better than to anger them. So as far as they're concerned, he can have the rest of Alariss.'

Ignus nodded. 'And even if Vayn was insane

enough to attack this Citadel – well, just look at it!'

Quinn understood. It wasn't just the Citadel's walls that protected it, but the mountain itself. The only land routes up to the Citadel were narrow paths up the sides of sheer cliffs. An army could hold out for years in comfort, living off the huge food stores, while their attackers froze and starved and had arrows rain down upon them.

'Time to find the lord of the manor,' Ulric sniffed. 'We've got a dragon to knight.'

Ignus led the way and they soon climbed the bronze-runged ladder down the side of the grain store and entered the maze of streets.

It was well after dark now, but even by the light of the blue-burning alchemical street lamps, the city took Quinn's breath away. Thea, too, looked around in awe as they moved from one column-lined street to the next. Tall stained-glass windows shed rainbow light from inside the buildings. Bridges and walkways draped the group with occasional shadows. Pale carven stone, rich indigo tiles and shining gold leaf blazed from all sides. It was a far cry from the poverty of Quinn's village, Rivervale, on the island of Yaross.

Sentries stood outside the larger buildings, keeping watch in the silence. They nodded politely as the group went past, but Quinn noticed that their hands never strayed from their sword hilts.

The central white tower soon loomed over the rooftops, so close that Quinn could make out the detail on the ornamental stonework. Suddenly a thought struck him. 'So that's where we're going?'

Ignus nodded. 'Nord's ancestral home. He likes to be up among the clouds.'

Quinn thought this over. 'He's a Storm Dragon type, right?'

'Oh, yes. He has – *had* – control over the winds and rain. Once he destroyed an entire army camp single-handedly with gales and floods. I've even seen him call down lightning before. It was devastating.'

When they reached the shadow of the White Tower, they passed a sentry guarding the main gate. He eyed the group suspiciously, until a drowsy look came over him suddenly and his eyes clamped shut like they'd been dragged down by heavy weights.

'Just a little something I picked up from my spell book,' Thea laughed.

'I think you're getting a bit too good at that,' Ignus said warily.

As they made their way through the gate and towards the tower, two vast doors of witch-oak loomed ahead of them. Quinn reckoned it would take a battering ram to get them open.

Ignus pounded on the doors with a heavy fist. High up in the tower, a light flickered into life.

Quinn watched as the light passed across a darkened window. Moments later, it passed across a window in the next floor down, then one in the floor below that, as if a great spiral staircase was steadily being descended.

Eventually the sound of metal locks clunking filled the air, and the doors to the tower creaked open. A hollow-cheeked man with pouchy eyes and a ridiculous wig peered out wearily.

'Yes?'

'We're here to see your master,' Ignus said gruffly.

The man raised an eyebrow and pursed his lips. 'Are you indeed? I'm afraid the master has far better things to do at this hour than to open his home to the likes of you. Good day.'

He tried to push the door shut, but Ignus shoved his foot in the way. 'We are Nord's old comrades,' he said through clenched teeth, throwing off his cloak. 'I think he'd want to know that Ignus and Ulric are here.'

The man made a face as if he'd trodden in something. 'I see. Well, I hope you're not expecting lavish hospitality. We had no word of your arrival . . .'

'We'll be fine.' Ignus pushed the door open and barged into the entrance hall. The man stumbled backwards into the hallway.

'Well, I never . . .' he began. 'Listen here, I'm Master Peter de Witt, major-domo, servant to the House of Nord, and I demand —'

De Witt's voice trailed off as a puff of smoke blasted out of Ignus's nostrils.

Quinn understood that the argument was over and stared in wonder as he entered the cavernous room. From carpet to ceiling, the walls were panelled in varnished wood hung with ancient-looking bows, swords, halberds and maces. In between the displays hung portraits: women and men with similar features and old-fashioned garments looked archly down on the visitors.

Cowering at the far end under a wall-mounted boar's head was a young man with watery eyes and a sickly, pale face. He swallowed hard as he saw the group approach.

'Is anyone going to take our things?' Ignus demanded gruffly.

'Morton will take them,' said De Witt, clearly still ruffled by the encounter, jerking a thumb at the cringing lad. 'But you must wait here. And touch *nothing*.'

Thea tossed Morton her travelling pack. The boy staggered and almost fell under the weight.

'Can you manage?' Thea frowned. 'You don't look well.'

Morton gave a gurgling sniff. 'Got a chill,

miss, that's all. I'll shake it off in a few days.'

De Witt strode up the wide staircase to the next floor and vanished from sight. Morton tottered after him. With nothing else to do, Quinn and Thea strolled around the hall and looked at the riches on display.

'See the size of that crossbow?' Thea whispered. 'And the barbed bolts? What in hell would you hunt with that?'

'One of those?' Quinn pointed to a mounted, stuffed head the size of a barrel. The scaly, ape-like creature had one goggling glass eye and a horn like a rhino.

Leaving Thea to marvel at the monster, he wandered over to a marble statue of a young woman. She was kneeling with her hands cupped as if she was drinking from a brook.

He was about to move on, but the statue's beauty transfixed him. She had a strange wildness to her; her hair was in disarray and she was glancing up as if listening for something. Quinn wondered if she was a nature spirit.

'Where is he?' complained Ulric after ten

minutes had passed without any sign of Nord. 'I'm starving.'

As if on cue De Witt appeared at the top of the stairs. 'The master will see you now. Follow me.'

The group headed through a grand upper gallery, where mirrors threw back the reflections of standing silver candelabras, and entered a long dining hall. All of the seats were empty, save for the one at the head of the table.

'Ignus? Ulric?' Nord stood up. 'Winds and stars, it *is* you!'

Quinn looked up at the man in front of him. He was tall and broad, with long black hair that was gathered back in a braid; he looked much younger than Quinn had expected. His grey silk gown hung so loose you could easily see his powerful arms and chest. *Those are a bowman's muscles,* Quinn thought, remembering all the splendid weapons that hung in the main hall ... and there, around Nord's ankle, was the copper manacle fastened by Vayn all those years ago.

Nord gave Ignus and Ulric a hearty greeting,

clasping their arms at the wrist, warrior-fashion. He kissed Thea's hand graciously, leaving her wide-eyed. But when he turned to Quinn, he did not even offer a hand to shake. He looked him up and down with cold, grey eyes, and soon turned back to his fellow Dragon Knights.

'Well, old friends,' Nord said. 'You cannot have climbed the Winter Mountain just to raid my mead cellar. So what business brings you here?'

'The noblest business of all,' said Ignus, showing the pale skin on his ankle where the manacle had once been. 'Freedom for us and for all of Alariss. And justice for Marek.'

Nord stepped back. A thin smile played on his lips, and he raised an eyebrow in doubt. 'And how exactly do you expect to do that?'

Ignus smiled proudly and put his hands on Quinn's shoulders, presenting him like a father would. 'The power of the true heir to the imperial line. Nord, this is Quinn: Marek's son. And our hope!'

Nord's face was an expressionless mask. 'How wonderful.' He stretched, the silk gown rippling over his muscles. 'Well, I expect you're tired after your journey. Perhaps we should talk further in the morning.' He snapped his fingers. 'Morton, be a good lad and see our guests to their chambers, would you?'

As the sickly-looking valet opened the door, Nord turned his back on the group and stood looking into the flames of the hearth.

Quinn and Thea traded glances. The shocked look on her face told him she was as surprised as he was.

'What are you talking about, Nord? We're not tired, damn it,' Ignus burst out. 'Don't you understand who Quinn is? He's the trueborn Emperor! He can set you free! You could enter dragonform again. Regain your powers. Be a Dragon Knight once more!'

'*Enough!*' Nord snapped.

Ignus stepped back in shock. Quinn bunched his eyebrows in confusion. The flames in the hearth crackled away, and all around silence descended on the room.

'Morton . . .' Nord whispered.

Morton coughed and ushered the group out of the room as best he could. 'If you'd all come this way, please.'

Quinn was about to say something but Ulric laid a warning hand on his shoulder. His head was spinning as he followed Morton out of the room, while Nord remained staring deeply into the fire.

What Quinn had seen made no sense. After twelve years in bondage, Nord the Dragon Knight had finally been offered his freedom ... and it looked as if he couldn't care less.

CHAPTER 3
THE RELUCTANT DRAGON

Quinn woke up feeling strange. For a minute he wondered what the pleasant, cosy sensation was that enveloped him from head to toes.

Warmth! he thought, eventually. He'd almost forgotten what that was like.

He sat up and looked around. He was in a four-poster bed heaped with blankets − gold and purple cushions scattered across the floor where he'd flung them in his sleep. After endless nights camped out on the cold, hard ground, this place was paradise.

He looked around for his clothes, and his

happy-sleepy mood vanished in a sudden panic. They were gone.

'Stolen?' He wondered out loud.

He felt under the pillow for his sword. It was still there. *At least if I have to go down to breakfast naked, I'll be armed . . .*

Wait, he told himself. *Morton probably took those clothes away to be washed.*

Sure enough, at the foot of the bed fresh clothes had been laid out for him. He breathed a sigh of relief. 'Just my size,' Quinn said to himself, slipping on a white silk shirt and some clean trousers. There was even a full-length mirror to admire himself in, if he wanted.

Still, something wasn't right. All this luxury and a good night's sleep ought to have put him in a fine mood, but the memory of Nord's behaviour set him on edge. Why had he looked at Quinn with such cold disinterest? And why hadn't he welcomed the possibility of freedom? Now Quinn had felt the joy and power of his own dragonform, he couldn't imagine why anyone could bear to be shut out from it.

Maybe it was nothing. He might have imagined it. Or perhaps Nord had just been grumpy from staying up too late last night. Quinn shrugged, pulled on the rest of his clothes and headed down the spiral stairs of the tower.

It soon became obvious as he walked through the hall: Quinn hadn't imagined it. Once again, Nord sat at the far end of the table, while Morton the valet ushered Quinn, Thea, Ignus and Ulric to their places at the other end. Any further from his lordship and they'd have to yell to make themselves heard.

Morton looked even worse this morning. He wasn't just pale, he was *white* – it was as if he'd been left alone with a hundred leeches overnight. But he still did his duty, piling bacon, eggs and spiced bean mush onto plates, his hands trembling.

Ulric tucked in right away, before Morton had finished loading his plate. 'Great spread,' he said, chewing a mouthful of eggs. 'Nord always knew how to lay on the hospitality for his brother Dragon Knights. Right, Ignus?'

'Right,' Ignus nodded, and tore a loaf of bread in half.

'Thank you. I will pass on your compliments to the cooks,' said Nord coolly.

Thea and Quinn exchanged glances. Quinn badly wanted to ask Nord why on earth he was so moody, but thought better of it. Best to let Ignus and Ulric do the talking. He bit into a warm cinnamon cake and chewed slowly, watching Nord all the while. The grey-clad man's expression never changed.

Ignus eventually cleared his throat. 'Nord, on the matter of the Dragon Knights –'

'Those were good times,' Nord interrupted. 'I will always treasure their memory.'

Were? thought Quinn.

'Damn it, man, don't you see that we're needed?' Ignus bellowed and thumped his fist on the table. Nord's fine china rattled. 'Quinn here can restore your knighthood and your powers with it. You can be a Dragon Knight again!'

'So you said last night. I believe you. But why would I want that?'

Unable to keep quiet any more, Quinn yelled, 'To fight Vayn, of course!'

Nord looked down at his manacle – then looked at Quinn directly for the first time. 'You are forgetting something, young man.'

'And what would that be?' Quinn asked.

'We've already fought Vayn once,' Nord said quietly. 'The Dragon Knights fell that day. Vayn won. We lost.'

A silence descended upon the room. Only Ulric was brave enough to break it.

'I've always admired your family crest, Nord,' he said, gesturing to the banner that hung on the wall. It showed a wild boar rearing up in front of the White Tower. 'But I think you might need to add something.'

'Oh? What would that be?' Nord asked.

'A big fat yellow streak right down the middle,' Ulric snorted.

Nord stood up. His chair fell back with a bang.

Quinn braced himself and Thea took a sharp breath. Any second now there would be a bust-up.

But Nord just stood there breathing heavily, and then closed his eyes. 'My gallant Dragon Knights, tell me this. If this boy strikes off my manacle and I join you, what do you hope to achieve?'

He paced back and forth, his hands clasped behind his back. 'We may be lonely up here in the Auric Citadel, but we have agents on all the islands to watch and report. What we have heard is deeply troubling. Vayn *knows* about you and your noble crusade. We have heard reports of Vayn's castle being reinforced, huge swathes of troops being mobilised, and every island of Alariss being locked down. Even the Citadel of Auric could be under threat!'

'That all just proves that Vayn's scared!' Thea put in. 'With good reason!'

'You asked us what we hope to achieve,' Ulric said. 'It's straightforward enough. We prove to the people they were fooled and that we Dragon Knights were a force for good, and we raise an army to take on Vayn and the Black Guard. We have the Emperor's own son on our side. The heir we were sworn to protect.'

Nord sat in silence for a while. Then he gave a long, exhausted sigh. 'No . . . no. Too much has changed, too much has been lost.'

'You are a Dragon Knight,' Ignus insisted.

'I *was* a Dragon Knight. Now I am only an exile, and Lord of the White Tower.'

'Poor you,' Ulric said, with heavy sarcasm. 'Stuck here with all this wealth and luxury. I thought Ignus and I had it rough.'

Nord had the decency to look shamefaced at that. He turned away.

'I could knight you right now,' said Quinn. 'With your powers, you could unleash the storm against Vayn. Think what a difference that would make. There are people all across Alariss who are suffering under him. People you could save. They need you!'

'The people of the Auric Citadel need protection too.' Nord stood up. 'I will not stand in your way, but I will not bring down Vayn's wrath on my city either.'

Quinn's mind ached from trying to argue with Nord. He wasn't telling the full story. Any fool could see that. *What did he mean, 'Too much has been lost'?*

The sound of the door creaking open disturbed the stony silence. De Witt entered the room, bringing a waft of perfume in with him.

'My lord, the archery practice court is ready.'

'Excellent!' For the first time since they'd arrived, Nord seemed to come alive, shoving his breakfast dishes aside and wiping his hands clean on a cloth. He noticed Quinn and the others looking blank, and explained: 'The Blood Moon festival is only days away. I'm competing in the archery event. You'll come and cheer me on, I hope?'

You must be joking, Quinn thought sourly.

'The lunar eclipse!' Thea burst out. 'I've read about it.'

'Indeed,' Nord said with a smile. 'Every ten years, the Blood Moon rises over the Winter Mountain, bringing with it the possibility of great good fortune. But the gods will only reward us if we prove worthy. So we hold a festival to find the best duellist, the best archer, the best jouster . . .'

Quinn clenched his fist under the table. It was hard to contain his anger. Obviously, as far as Nord was concerned, the conversation about Vayn was over.

Ulric perked up. 'Did you say jousting? I might have to put my name down for that.'

Nord laughed. 'Now there's the Ulric I remember! Oh gods, the fields of Terragorn. You nearly shattered my spine!'

Ulric turned to Quinn. 'Back when Nord first joined us, he was a bit ... well ... he had a stick up his backside, so to speak. Not his fault. His family's old and rich. So we tried to get him to have a bit of fun.'

Nord told Quinn, 'All the Dragon Knights jousted against one another. We were black and blue by the end of it.'

'On horses?' Quinn asked.

'No!' Ignus chuckled. 'On *each other!* We took it in turns to enter dragonform, and rode on one another's backs. Kyria got a lance up her nose . . .'

The three Dragon Knights began to talk about

old times. Quinn sat to one side, stewing in his own private thoughts. How could Nord care about something as mundane as an archery competition when Vayn – the tyrant who'd beaten and humiliated him – still sat on the Imperial Throne?

An icy cold draught on the back of Quinn's neck made him shudder. He turned to see Morton come wobbling into the room, looking sicker than ever. The valet leaned forward to take Quinn's empty plate, but the movement overbalanced him and he toppled over like a felled tree.

The servant didn't get up. He rolled over onto his back with a gasp. Quinn saw what had happened to the young man's face and instinctively sprang away from him. His hand went to his sword.

'Nord!' he yelled. 'Something's happening!'

Morton's eyes had turned a blank, frozen blue-white. The pupils had vanished completely. A seeping white mist crept from his mouth and nostrils. His body jerked and twitched randomly, like a puppet with an angry child yanking the strings.

'Dear gods,' Thea said. 'Something's sucking the life right out of his body.'

Quinn and Thea looked on in horror. The servant's heels drummed on the floorboards. A dry death rattle sounded in his throat. The last of his life force came seething out of his mouth . . .

CHAPTER 4

MOUNTAIN CHILL

'Don't just stand there gawping, get him up off the floor!' Nord ordered. 'De Witt? Where are you?'

De Witt came running up the stairs, his wig bobbing up and down as if he were some ludicrous bird. 'My lord?'

'Run and fetch the doctor. Now!'

De Witt scurried away. Nord stood back, arms folded, while Quinn and Ignus each took one of Morton's arms. They hoisted him up and across the room to a chair that stood against the wall.

Quinn's hand touched the flesh of Morton's

forearm. He flinched. The servant was so cold he was painful to touch. 'A corpse hacked out of a glacier wouldn't be as cold as this!' he gasped. 'How's he still alive?'

'I'm not sure he *is* alive,' said Thea warily. 'Look at his eyes. People are not supposed to look like that!'

Morton was still twitching, his eyes ghostly blank marbles. Now his face was turning blue – not the bluish pallor of someone who's been out in the cold, but a ghastly supernatural blue, like a coal flame.

Quinn glanced over at Nord. The man kept his distance, gripping the back of a chair, his own face ghostly pale. Quinn guessed there was nothing supernatural about *his* pallor. He was clearly afraid.

'Nord! We have to do something!' Quinn yelled.

'I have. The doctor will be here soon,' Nord snapped.

'We can't wait that long. Thea, what about magic? Cast a spell. Help him.'

'I can't,' she said, sounding helpless. 'Without

knowing the cause, I can't find the cure. I could kill him, or worse.'

Ignus leaned forward and took hold of Morton's violently shaking hands. 'The lad's cold, so let's warm him up.' He took a deep breath through his nose and furrowed his brow in concentration.

In human form, Ignus could use his flame-dragon magic in careful, controlled ways. Quinn felt heat rippling from the big man. It radiated down Ignus's arms and into Morton's body.

Like a retreating tide, the frost-blue pallor crept back from his fingertips, crawled down his hands and back up his arms. It was astonishing to watch. Before Quinn's eyes, Morton was becoming human once more.

The boy coughed a human-sounding cough. He blinked; his eyes were wet and bloodshot but slowly returning to normal. 'Wh-who am I?' he gasped.

'You're in the tower, and you're safe,' Nord assured him. He sounded a lot calmer all of a sudden. 'Margery Devereux is on her way. Just keep still.'

Quinn threw Nord an angry glance. 'What's going on?'

'Nothing to worry about. Morton's just got a spot of the mountain chill.'

'He didn't even know who he was!'

'He said "where am I", not "who". He's a little delirious, but that happens. Mountain chill is an old affliction up here in these heights. People have gone down with it for as long as the Auric Citadel has been here.'

He didn't say 'where', thought Quinn. *He said 'who'*. But he didn't get a chance to argue. Nord had turned away and begun quietly talking to Thea, leading her by the arm to a high window. He was saying something about mountain folk-lore: frost grubkins and rime weasels. Thea, wide-eyed, drank it all in.

The doors flew open and De Witt bundled an old woman into the room. 'Found her,' he gasped, and sank into a comfortable chair. He tugged out a huge scarlet handkerchief and mopped his brow with it.

Quinn guessed this odd-looking little woman

must be the doctor. She had a deranged look to her, with staring eyes and wild white hair spiralling off in all directions, but the smile she gave him was kindly. She looked eagerly up at him. 'Well, young man, where's my patient?'

'Over here.' Quinn led her to Morton.

The doctor rubbed her hands together briskly and poked Morton in the ribs, making him yelp. Despite looking like she must be a hundred years old, she seemed full of energy. 'Touch of the mountain chill, is it? Not surprised, lots of it about.' She jabbed a finger at Ignus and Ulric. 'You two look like fine, strong chaps. Pick this laddie up and carry him for me, quick sharp.'

'Where are you taking him?' Quinn asked.

'Somewhere he can recover! Plenty of bed rest, that's what a mountain-chill victim needs!'

Quinn tried to ask what the 'mountain chill' actually *was,* but the doctor ignored him. The two Dragon Knights picked Morton up between them and hauled him out of the room. The doctor bustled along behind. Once the bizarre procession was out of sight, Nord turned to Quinn and Thea, smiling awkwardly.

'My apologies for the drama,' he said. 'Poor lad. Don't trouble yourselves about him, he'll be fine.'

Quinn wasn't convinced; it was clear Nord was just trying to change the subject.

'In fact, why don't you both join me for archery practice?' Nord continued. 'There's no use sticking around here.'

'I haven't really used a bow much before,' Quinn said.

'Then practice is exactly what you need.' Nord patted him heartily on the shoulder. 'What do you say?'

Quinn and Thea glanced at each other with concern. Nord was a little too eager to brush off Morton's sickness for Quinn's liking, and suddenly interested in him for no apparent reason. Quinn was suspicious, but for now he reckoned it would be best to just do as Nord pleased and get to the bottom of things later.

He looked up at Nord as eagerly as he could muster. 'Lead the way,' he said.

Nord took them through to the courtyard behind the White Tower. A beautiful private walled garden stretched out ahead of them, where paved paths threaded through snow-covered lawns. The cold air was sharp with the scent of pine and mountain flowers.

Here and there stood white marble statues of the gods. They looked as majestic and lordly as they could under an inch of fallen snow. Quinn guessed the same master sculptor who had created the statue of the young woman in Nord's hall had made them. As he watched, a raven fluttered and perched on the head of Nyretha, the Goddess of Music.

Odd, Quinn thought. Nord kept the gods themselves out in the snow and rain, while a common woman stood indoors among his other treasures. *Maybe she's some sort of personal goddess.*

'It's an impressive spot,' Thea said.

'So I'm told,' said Nord, strolling over to a

wooden table on which a selection of longbows and arrows had been carefully laid. Next to them was a deep copper bowl of mulled honey-coloured tea that steamed invitingly. Nord filled drinking horns for them all.

'Have you lived here all your life?' asked Quinn. He took a sip; the tea was spiced and burned like dragonfire. He coughed.

'Keeps the chill off, doesn't it?' said Nord with a smirk. 'Yes, I grew up here. Generations of us have. My family was one of the first to settle the Winter Mountain.'

Nord showed them where the archery targets had been set up. He explained how the first of his forefathers, Eremith, had been the sentinel who kept watch over the mountain camp. 'He was a legend among bowmen. Nothing, not wolf nor troll nor ice-lich, dared come close to the camp while Eremith was in his watchtower. Two shots were all he needed. The first shot was a warning. The second went through the heart.'

'Watchtower?' said Quinn, glancing up at the White Tower behind them.

Nord guessed his meaning and nodded. 'The White Tower now stands where Eremith's watch-tower once stood. We've all been trained to the bow since Eremith's time.' He picked up a longbow and plucked the string. It sang like a harp.

'Your whole family were trained archers?' Thea asked.

'Every one.'

'But where are they all?'

'Gone, now,' Nord said. 'Scattered to the four winds, dead and forgotten on foreign shores. My Uncle Hengir, who raised me, died fighting Vayn's men. I have no children . . . and no wife to bear me any. I am the last of my line.'

'I'm sorry,' Thea said.

Nord shrugged. 'Why? All men die. Only our honour lives on. Now the Blood Moon festival is almost here, it's my turn to represent our family's honour in the archery contest.'

Quinn took another swig of hot tea. 'I guess shooting at straw targets must feel pretty tame compared to trolls and ice-liches,' he said boldly.

Nord gave him a dangerous look. 'The festival

is a serious matter. Ten years of good luck depends on it.'

And while you waste your time with superstitions and festivals the rest of Alariss is burning, thought Quinn. But he kept the thought to himself. 'So let's shoot,' he said.

It wasn't long before Quinn's arms were aching and grazed where the bow string had ripped his skin. A surprising number of his arrows had hit the target on or near the centre. But a lot had thunked into the ground or flown out of sight.

Nord was a deadly shot. Almost all his arrows were in the gold circle in the middle – the same height off the ground as a man's heart.

As Thea took her first shot, Quinn thought he saw her wiggle her fingers and whisper as she notched her arrow.

'Watch and learn,' she said with a wink. The arrow zipped through the air and stuck quivering in the gold.

Quinn clapped. Thea bent low to give Nord a sarcastic bow and stepped back so he could take his shot.

Nord notched his arrow and said coldly, 'No, madam. It is *you* who needs a lesson.' His eyes narrowed, and for an instant Quinn could swear he saw a stab of light in their grey depths, like lightning. The feathers on Nord's arrow ruffled, but there was no wind.

Quinn understood. *He's using his storm powers to boost his shot! That arrow's going to smash right through the target – and probably the wall behind it as well!*

Thea had seen it too. As Nord drew back his arm to fire, she moved her fingers and murmured something under her breath.

Nord loosed his shot. The arrow screamed as it flew, like a hurricane wind tearing around a rocky crag. But an invisible force nudged it in mid-flight. Instead of slamming into the target, it zoomed off at an angle and chipped the nose off a statue of Corgom, God of Law.

Nord turned on Thea furiously. 'You cheated! You've been using witchcraft!'

Thea just laughed. 'And using dragonblood powers is playing fair, is it, your lordship?'

Nord reddened. 'That is different. My dragon-blood is well known. You kept your magic hidden from me until now.'

Quinn had had enough. 'So you'll use your powers to win archery contests, but not to fight Vayn?' he shouted in Nord's face. 'I don't get it! Why won't you come with us? Why don't you want to be a Dragon Knight?'

Nord seemed like he was about to say something important. Then he sighed deeply and pressed his knuckled fist to his forehead. 'I have said more than enough on the matter already. I will say no more.'

'Fine.' Quinn turned on his heel. 'Come on, Thea. Let's just go and find the next Knight. We're wasting our time with this one.'

Thea caught his arm. 'Wait! Let's stay until the festival, at least. We could even enter the archery competition. You're a good shot.'

'I suppose.'

'So challenge Nord! Who knows what you might win?'

Quinn hesitated. Then a slow smile spread

over his face. Thea smiled too as she saw he'd caught on to her idea.

'All right,' he said. 'I'll enter the contest – if Nord's willing to take a wager.'

Nord looked up. 'Wager?'

'If I win the archery contest, I knight you and you come with us. If I lose, we leave and we never bother you again.'

Nord let out a harsh laugh. 'I salute your audacity, lad, though we both know what the outcome will be.' Nord, supremely confident, didn't hesitate. 'I accept!'

CHAPTER 5

DARKNESS RETURNS

The next day, Ignus shook Quinn awake just after dawn. 'Rise and shine! You and I are heading down to the Citadel.'

'Urgh.' Quinn groaned. 'Why?'

'Doctor's orders. Margery needs some orris root and cinder seeds to make a tonic for young Morton. I said we'd fetch them. There's bound to be an apothecary in the Citadel.'

'Tell her to send De Witt.' Quinn liked the idea of that snide, slimy man being out of the White Tower for a while.

'He's busy with festival preparations. Besides,

you could do with a walk around the Citadel. They're your people, remember, *Your Majesty.*'

Quinn winced, still unable to get used to his new status. 'If you say so.'

'That's the spirit. I'll let you get dressed.'

Soon after, the pair of them headed out through the huge front doors and Quinn got his first proper look at the Auric Citadel. For a boy who had grown up poor, with his aunt doing back-breaking laundry work to bring in a few measly coins, it was a shock to see so much wealth on display.

All the streets were freshly swept. There were no beggars. Shop-window glass shone like soap bubbles in the morning light. The citizens were out, greeting one another as they passed, or sitting outside taverns consuming hot foamy drinks and chatting. They were all dressed like rich merchants, with high collars, lacy frills and silken tunics. Quinn stared at the people who could have been mistaken for royalty in another land. Golden ornaments twined around their shoulders and rings glittered on their fingers.

Many of the men wore as much jewellery as the women, though the gold they wore was chunky and heavy. The fashion seemed to be a sort of twisted golden rope that draped around the neck. Some of the men carried swords, but they were so encrusted with gems that they'd be hard to fight with. Quinn guessed they were just for show. The mercenary guards on the street corners had the real weapons.

Ignus spotted a man with an especially fancy rapier go by. 'What's the point of a pretty toy like that? Honest steel, that's what folk need.'

'I guess this place has been secure for so long, they've forgotten what swords are for.'

'That's just it!' Ignus said disgustedly. 'The Auric Citadel has *never* been attacked. Who'd be fool enough to try?'

'Someone who wanted to steal their riches?'

'Impossible,' said Ignus. 'Even if you brought a whole army, they'd never make it up this high.'

A man's cough caught Quinn's attention. He looked pale and sickly, much like Morton had.

Quinn glanced around and saw other pale faces in the crowds.

'I guess you can't keep disease away with swords and high walls,' he said. 'Money can't buy everything.'

They turned a corner into a street full of craft shops. The windows displayed gorgeous goods: carvings in pale golden wood, replica longboats with proud dragons at the prow, mountain foxes and hares in gold and silver.

'So why did Nord think the Citadel might be under threat?' Quinn asked. 'I thought Vayn was leaving the Citadel well alone.'

Ignus's face darkened. 'It is true, Vayn's tentacles have but a weak grip here. But Nord knows that high walls and isolation cannot always protect what he holds dear.'

Quinn stopped in his tracks. 'You *know*, don't you?'

'Keep moving,' grunted Ignus.

'No. Not until you tell me what the big secret is.'

'I've said too much already. Nord is a brother, he deserves respect –'

'Spit it out, Ignus! Why is Nord being so difficult?'

Ignus let out a long, heavy sigh. 'That would have a lot to do with Catherine.'

Finally, thought Quinn. 'Go on.'

'Catherine was Nord's betrothed,' Ignus told him. 'They'd known each other since they were children. You'd have liked her, Quinn. She was noble born, an academic. Yet, she was tough. She had a mean swing with a sword and could swear to make a soldier blush.'

Quinn laughed. 'What happened to her?'

'Some said she died, but no one knows. You see, when Vayn stripped us of our powers and exiled us, Nord came back here to the White Tower. You wouldn't think it to listen to him now, but he was hell-bent on vengeance back then. He had all sorts of crazy plans: he said he'd raise an army, and wanted to use the Citadel as a base from which to strike against Vayn, that kind of thing. But when he came home and he found that Catherine was gone, it broke his spirit.'

Ignus told Quinn the tale of Nord's tragic homecoming. Catherine had disappeared from the White Tower overnight. Nobody ever saw her again. Nord's rage eventually gave way to grief, and grief to resignation.

'According to some, Catherine heard Nord had been killed fighting Vayn, and flung herself off the Citadel walls in despair,' said Ignus. 'They even wrote a ballad about it.'

Quinn felt he understood Nord now and remembered what he'd said just the day before: '*I have no children, and no wife to bear me any.*' No wonder he was in pain.

'So nobody knows what happened to her?'

Ignus shook his head. 'Nord lost *everything* that day. His dragonblood powers, his knight-hood, his Emperor and his betrothed.'

'So, Catherine . . . was she the woman in Nord's hall?'

'The statue's of her, aye. It was a gift to seal

their engagement. He sings to her, De Witt told me. Sits up at night and sings the old songs she used to love . . .' Ignus fell silent.

Up ahead was an archway formed by the spread wings of two griffin statues, one on each side of the street. Their talons and feathers shone with gold – one of Alariss's many bizarre and monstrous creatures that had been immortalised in stone.

Beyond lay the market square. Quinn could smell it before he saw it. The mind-fuddling mixture of odours made his head spin, like an orchestra with each instrument playing a different song.

He breathed in the rich smell of hot honey from a mead seller's stall mingling with the delicious fug of milk and sizzling batter from a pancake maker nearby. With it came the oily mineral tang of metal from an ironwright, the woolly whiff of sheepskins from a parchment seller and a dark smell like fireworks and liquorice from the potion brewer. All of them, and dozens more, called out their wares to anyone who would buy.

'So, what are we looking for?' Quinn asked, confused.

'Each trade has a symbol,' Ignus began. 'See how each stall has a board – an anvil there, look, and a scroll there? Look for the sign of an eye in a five-pointed star. That's the symbol magic suppliers use.'

'Oh. Like that guy?' Quinn pointed at a lean man in a hooded robe, standing behind a table covered with curious items: a candle shaped like a human hand, a crystal that slowly cycled through colours, a jar packed to the brim with eyes, and piles of roots and herbs. Around his neck hung the star-and-eye symbol.

'Perfect!'

The merchant smiled to see them, and his smile widened even further when Ignus brought out his pouch of gold. The price he asked made Quinn choke. A tiny packet of orris root and cinder seeds cost as much as a horse and cart back in Yaross, but as Ignus pointed out, people in the Citadel could easily afford those prices.

'No wonder they're all rich, if that's how they do business,' Quinn muttered.

As they were walking away, a shrill, inhuman scream rang out.

Quinn looked around, thinking one of the merchants had been robbed and wondering if maybe they deserved it. But the crowds in the market square were all looking in the same direction: up.

Above them, an eagle was circling. It was close enough for its wingtips to brush the rooftops. It screeched again.

As Quinn watched, it swept down with claws outstretched. People screamed and ran out of the way. 'Shoot it, just shoot it!' one woman shrieked.

Pampered, sheltered fools can't even cope with a wild bird, thought Quinn. *It's hungry, that's all. This lot don't know what that's like.*

But instead of circling and swooping, the eagle was flapping its wings with aggression. It wasn't on the lookout for food. 'Something's wrong,' Ignus said. 'It's not just hunting, it's on the attack. Look!'

As the eagle flew up again, only to begin another vicious dive, Quinn could see that Ignus was right. The eagle ignored the hunks of smoked meat that hung from the butcher's stall and instead sunk its claws into the butcher himself. The people scattered, screaming and yelling.

One of the Citadel guards raised a crossbow and took careful aim. The eagle screeched and plunged yet again. The guard fired, but the bolt went whirring off into the sky. Cursing, the guard began to fumble a new bolt into the notch.

'Nord could have bullseyed it,' Quinn muttered.

'This lot are no use,' Ignus agreed. 'Looks like it's down to us.'

Quinn pulled out his sword, the golden heirloom from his royal father. Instantly the dagger-sized weapon flashed into full size.

An agonised shriek went up. The eagle's claws had finally drawn blood. It had clamped its long talons into a hapless priest's shoulder and it wasn't letting go. It beat its wings in a flurry of wild feathers, snapping at the few citizens who dared to come close. Red rivulets ran down the priest's white robe.

'Get out of the way!' Quinn yelled to the milling citizens.

With a roar he charged the flailing eagle. Sensing danger, it released the priest, only to lunge at Quinn instead. A nightmarish head suddenly filled his vision, the beak sharp as a meat hook, ripping and tearing at his eyes and face.

Horror gripped him. The eagle's eyes were all wrong. They were a solid, frosty blue. Just like Morton's had been. A weird, white mist smoked from its beak.

Quinn lashed out with his sword, striking into what felt like feathers but was oddly without substance. The eagle screamed high and shrill. It clawed furiously at him and Quinn felt a hot, searing pain rip down his arm. A wet flow of blood tickled the back of his hand.

He raised his arm to slash at the eagle again, but before he could land a blow, it wheeled back into the air and went sailing up past the tops of the towers.

'No,' Quinn said. 'You don't get away that easily!' He flung his sword to one side and launched himself into the air, the dragonblood coursing through his veins in a blazing rush. The transformation took only seconds this time, and soon Ignus and the other citizens were small specks on the ground. Quinn never even touched the ground; his dragon wings were out and beating before gravity could claim him, powering him up in pursuit.

Quinn flapped his wings ferociously and soared between the Citadel's high towers. He opened his strong dragon's jaw and let out a lick of flame. Just as he closed in on the eagle, it dived once again, using Quinn's huge size against him.

The eagle was smaller and faster, and more used to the sky. Quinn lunged after it, trying to catch up, but it rushed around the curve of the mountain and vanished from sight. He let out a roar of frustration, and then headed back down to the firm ground of the Citadel.

Ignus and the priest watched him approach.

Quinn resumed human form in front of them and glanced at the circle of awed onlookers that had formed. He picked up the sword that he'd flung to the ground.

'Nice try,' Ignus rumbled.

'Not good enough, though,' Quinn panted. 'I should have had it.'

'At least it's gone now,' Ignus said.

'Dragonblooded one,' the priest interrupted hoarsely. He was trembling all over. 'I owe you my life.'

'It's nothing,' Quinn said, still panting. He turned to the crowd. 'One of you, get this man a bandage! Can't you see he's hurt?'

While someone ran off to fetch a healer, the priest beckoned Quinn close. Quinn saw his eyes were wide with fright. He wasn't just trembling from the pain and shock. He was *terrified*.

'That was not an ordinary bird,' the priest whispered.

'I know. I saw. Do you know what it was?'

'Dark times are upon us.' The priest's voice quavered, his eyes darting left and right. He licked his dry lips, almost afraid to speak. 'They are back . . . the hungry ones; the ancient ones. *The mountain spirits of Auric have returned!'*

CHAPTER 6

THE GOLDEN LIBRARY

Back at the White Tower, Quinn and Ignus braced themselves to encounter De Witt. Quinn went to bang on the door, expecting they'd have to wait for the major-domo to let them in, but to their amazement the door was flung open before Quinn laid a hand on it.

'About time you got back!' Thea grabbed Quinn by the arm and dragged him inside. 'You won't believe what I've found, it'll take your . . .' she hesitated. 'Quinn, your arm –'

Thea looked at the fresh blood on her fingers from Quinn's clawed arm and saw the grim look on his face. She let go, wincing in sympathy. 'That looks nasty.'

'It *is* nasty,' Ignus said.

'It's just a scratch,' Quinn told her, shaking off Ignus.

'Scratch? It looks like someone's raked you with a rusty nail! You might get lockjaw, or the flesh-rot, or worse. Hey, I know an old spell to purge the body – never tried it before – want me to cast it?'

'No thanks!' Quinn did *not* like the thought of being 'purged'. From what he knew, that would mean being violently sick . . . or worse.

'Try to talk some sense into him,' Ignus said, pushing his way past. 'I'll go and find Ulric and deliver Morton's medicine.'

Now that he was alone with Thea in the hall, Quinn quickly pointed out the statue of Catherine and explained who she was.

Thea gave a low whistle. 'So that's why our host's roosting up here like a melancholy raven! He's lost his lady love.'

'Better not talk like that in front of Ignus.

He'd say you were being disrespectful of Nord.'

'Nord's been moping up here for too long,' Thea said. 'Now tell me what gave you that "scratch".'

Quinn told her about the eagle in the market-place, and how its eyes had glowed blue, just like Morton's. 'The priest said something about mountain spirits returning, which seemed to make sense. Doesn't this whole place feel haunted to you?'

'Yeah. Not just by the ghosts of Nord's tragic past, either,' said Thea.

'Good to know it's not just me.' Quinn shuddered. Now he'd talked openly about the ominous feelings he was having, they came back twice as strong. Something about the White Tower just didn't sit right.

Thea grabbed him – by the uninjured arm this time – and began to drag him up the stairs. 'Come on. I told you I'd found something incredible. You need to see this.'

'What is it?'

'You'll see!'

'Just tell me, Thea. I've had enough surprises for one day.'

Thea turned to face him, her eyes shining. 'The library! Right at the top of the tower! It's just about the best library I've ever seen in my life.'

'Great. I'm happy for you.'

'That isn't even the best part!' Thea flailed her hands. 'The best part is what I've found in the *Drakkensbok*. Or to be more specific, what I haven't found. Just wait. It'll all make sense.'

By the time they reached the topmost floor, running past bedrooms, armouries, galleries, sunrooms and what looked like an alchemical laboratory, both of them were out of breath. Thea shoved the door open and gasped. 'Ta-daaa!'

Quinn was braced to be unimpressed. Thea was a book fiend, after all, and any library was heaven to her. But she hadn't exaggerated how stunning Nord's library was.

Looking up into the library tower was like staring up a chimney lined with books. Level after level rose up into the dizzying heights, all the way to the golden dome at the top of the tower. Each new section was divided from the rest by a curved balcony, with rickety rails connecting the whole thing together. It would be a nightmare for anyone who was afraid of heights.

'There must be a million and one books here!' Quinn said. He wondered if Eremith himself had started the library, centuries ago – it certainly looked like it would take a dozen lifetimes to assemble the collection.

'Over here,' Thea urged him. She led the way to a polished pantherwood reading table, as black and heavy-looking as an altar to the dark gods. Quinn saw she had already laid several books out, open.

An exciting possibility struck him. 'Are these spell books?'

'Oh, no. These are history books. And this big one here is the *Drakkensbok* of Friar Rupert. One of the most complete volumes of dragon lore in the world!'

The *Drakkensbok* had curling, golden pages

that were almost transparent. Colourful figures of dragons chased each other in the margins. It was a work of art.

'It looks amazing, but I don't get why you're so excited,' Quinn admitted.

'OK. We know you're an Earth Dragon type, because your father was one and you have the right kinds of powers. But one thing doesn't make sense. You know how when you go into dragonform you have golden scales?'

'Yeah, so?'

'So I've checked the *Drakkensbok*. Guess how many other golden Earth Dragons there have been in recorded history.'

Quinn shrugged.

'Zero. You're the first.'

'What? That can't be right. Check again.'

'Quinn, I've checked *three times!* All through history, Earth Dragons have been blue or grey or brown. There are records of hundreds of dragons here. They're always those three colours, never anything else. Never gold like you.'

Quinn was lost for words. *I'm not even used*

to being a dragonblood, he thought. *Now I can't even be a normal dragonblood? I have to be some golden freak?*

'I don't get it,' he said.

'Me neither,' said Thea. 'Anyway, there's something else I need to show you. You know that spell book Mrs Onyx gave me? I've been studying hard.'

Quinn laughed. 'You're not still jealous of my dragonblood powers, are you?'

'Maybe a little,' Thea grinned. 'After you made that stone bird and I made him fly, I had a brainwave. If I can lift a heavy stone bird with magic, then maybe . . .'

'Maybe what?'

Thea didn't answer. She sat down on the dusty library floor with her legs crossed and her hands resting on her knees. She closed her eyes and began murmuring softly.

Quinn looked around the room, waiting for something to start moving. He guessed Thea was going to lift one of the heavy lecterns or make the books float off the shelves. But to his amazement, it was Thea herself who slowly rose up from the floor.

'You're levitating!' Quinn shouted, impressed.

'You aren't ... the only one ... who can fly,' Thea muttered, her face twisted with the effort of concentration.

She went on rising, hovering in the air like a weightless soap bubble. Suddenly she dropped down a few feet, only to catch herself and begin floating steadily up again. 'Whoops. Nearly lost it there.'

'I probably shouldn't distract you, right?' Quinn teased.

'Ha! I make this look easy.' Thea kept going until she was almost under the crossbeams of the great golden dome, right at the top of the library. She whooped in triumph and her voice echoed down its chimney-like length.

Quinn felt uneasy. 'OK. I'm impressed. Come back down now.'

Thea didn't come back down. Concentrating even harder now, she slowly uncrossed her legs and stretched out her arms, then tilted herself forwards. Quinn held his breath as Thea tumbled over, somersaulting in mid-air.

He cheered and applauded – but then he saw she was still tumbling end over end. 'Whoa!' Thea yelled. 'Not so fast, not so fast . . .'

Her words didn't do any good. She was spinning faster, not slower. The more she panicked, the more the magic whirled her out of control. Clouds of dust billowed up from the tops of the bookshelves. Thea became a tumbling, yelling, spinning figure like a dangling ornament whacked by an angry child.

'Are you OK?' Quinn shouted.

'I'm fine! I've got this, I just need to boost the spell. *Verem, vita . . .*'

Swirling dust caught in Thea's throat. She burst out coughing before the spell was finished.

Next moment, as if an invisible cord had been cut, Thea fell.

She plunged down and grabbed desperately for something to hang onto. Luckily, she was close to one of the bookcases that lined the wall. She caught hold and clung on for dear life.

A low groan from the bookcase told Quinn that Thea wasn't safe just yet. Pulled off balance by the force of Thea's crash landing, it slowly tilted forwards and fell with a tremendous crash onto the balcony rail. The top shelves emptied their contents out over the edge.

Quinn stood paralysed with amazement as a rain of books showered down around him. A slow flurry of loose pages came wafting down after them, falling gently like autumn leaves. Lastly, descending from on high into the chaos like an apologetic angel, came Thea. Clearly she'd regained control of her magic, but it was far too late.

Thea and Quinn stood in a sea of papery disaster.

They stared at each other for a moment, too horrified to speak. Then they both burst out laughing at the same time.

'I guess I need to work on that one a little more,' Thea said. She sat down on a pile of books.

Quinn looked around at the devastation − then a large book with ornate metal fittings caught his eye. The front cover gleamed with mother-of-pearl and a stout clasp held it shut. It looked more like a treasure box than a book.

He waded through the heaps of fallen books and reached out a hand.

From behind him a furious voice roared: 'Fools! Trespassing idiots! What have you DONE?'

Quinn spun around. Nord stood there in the doorway, his face red and the veins standing out on his neck. Behind him cowered the doctor, Margery Devereux, with a bowl of steaming liquid in her hands.

'Oh, dear me,' she said, shaking her head. 'My patient isn't going to get better if you young ruffians keep making all these loud noises.'

'Never mind the damn noises,' spat Nord. 'Look at this place! Do you two imbeciles have any idea how much damage you've done?'

'It was my fault,' Thea stammered. 'I made Quinn come here, I wanted to show him . . .'

'The library is forbidden to you! You had no business here!' screamed Nord. Lightning flickered in his eyes.

Quinn stepped forward. 'We're sorry. We'll clear up the mess.'

'I have no use for your half-witted apologies,' Nord hissed. 'I offered you my hospitality, outlaws and fugitives that you are, and this is how you repay me? No more. Perhaps you should consider this your last night in the White Tower!'

Nord turned to leave. He slammed the doors behind him with a violent crash of thunder that shook the whole tower to its roots.

CHAPTER 7

SHADOWS IN THE NIGHT

The evening meal that night was not cheery.
The disaster in the library had created a grim
atmosphere. Not even Ulric's jokes about the
dodgy cooking could lift the mood. Thea and
Quinn shared guilty looks and Ignus glared
accusingly at them both.

Nord sat stony-faced at the end of the table,
not eating a mouthful. Nobody spoke a word.
Cutlery clinked in the silence.

Eventually, the cook came in to clear away the
plates herself, since Morton was still recovering
somewhere in the tower. Nord immediately rose

and stomped out of the room. Everybody sighed in relief to see him go.

'Thank the gods that's over,' Thea whispered to Quinn.

'So what do we do now?' he replied.

Ignus interrupted, 'We go to our rooms and we stay there until the morning. Understand?'

'Might be an idea to pack your things, too,' said Ulric sarcastically. 'We don't seem to be welcome here all of a sudden.'

The four of them trooped off to their respective guest rooms. Quinn's was past all the others, at the end of the corridor, overlooking the rear courtyard. One by one his companions left him, disappearing into their rooms, until he was walking alone.

He turned a corner and almost ran into De Witt, who was coming the other way. The man reared up like a snake and glared down at Quinn. His nostrils flared as if he smelled something disgusting.

Quinn coughed politely, but De Witt didn't move out of his way.

'Excuse me,' Quinn said through gritted teeth.

'On your way to smash up some more of my lord's possessions, are you?' De Witt sneered.

Quinn pondered shoving the man over onto his perfumed backside, but decided against it. There had been enough trouble today as it was.

He stepped around De Witt, giving him an evil look of his own, and opened the door to his room. The servant seemed in an especially foul mood tonight. Then Quinn had a thought: De Witt was probably on his way to clear up the book avalanche in the library. That explained why he was here, and why he had spoken to Quinn with such loathing.

Quinn stripped off his clothes and crawled into bed. He mulled over Thea's discovery of the *Drakkensbok* and the strange absence of golden Earth Dragons from the records. He wondered what else he might learn, until with a stab of guilt he realised that whatever secrets the library still held were lost to him forever. Nord would never allow him to set foot in that place again.

*

That night, as Quinn lay sleeping, disturbing dreams crept into his head. He was flying in pursuit of the eagle again, in his dragonform. Suddenly it was as if his dragon-wings were made of heavy granite, and he couldn't stay in the air. Flapping helplessly, he plunged towards the snowy peak of the Winter Mountain. He crashed down into the barren whiteness.

Quinn groaned and rolled over in bed. In his dreams, he rolled over in the snow and looked up into the bleak and empty sky. A low moaning filled his ears, like the wind blowing across the mountaintop.

Pale, transparent faces loomed above him, ugly and inhuman. They seemed to be carved out of some kind of ghostly ice. They had narrow, mean features, like the spirit-masks people had made thousands of years ago, and whispered to one another in a language Quinn couldn't understand.

Mountain spirits, he thought. He tried to move, but he was paralysed.

One of them bent down to peer into his face.

Its gaping black eyes filled his vision. Right in their midst burned two sparks of frosty blue, like stars made of ice.

Quinn woke up with a gasp. His heart was thumping wildly.

The moaning noise he'd heard in his dream was still going on. *It's just the wind,* he told himself, and tried to relax. *Nothing to worry about.*

Then, with a nasty shock, he realised the sound was coming from *inside* the tower. It was moving along the corridor. It was outside his own door.

Quinn lay stock still, his hands clenched into claws.

But the noise grew fainter, and the unseen thing moved away.

Quinn hesitated for a second. Then he flung back the bedclothes, crept to his door and opened it a crack – just enough to peer out.

A hunched figure, swathed in black, was edging down the ancient corridor. The moaning sound came from all around it, like a halo of ghosts. Quinn gripped the wood of the door, certain the figure would turn around at any moment and stare right at him.

But the figure kept going. It turned the corner and vanished from sight. Moments later, Quinn heard the steady *creak, creak, creak* as it ascended the stairs.

His heart pounding, Quinn followed. He'd left his bed wearing nothing but a long shirt and a loose pair of trousers, and his bare feet trod silently on the thickly carpeted stairs. The corridors were dark and silent, with only a feeble light coming in from the tall, slitted tower windows.

He thought for a minute he'd gone the wrong way, but then he caught a glimpse of the black-clad figure as it clambered up the steps ahead of him. He wondered where it was heading to, although in his heart he was certain he knew already.

Sure enough, when they reached the uppermost floors, the figure gently pushed the library doors open. Quinn kept his distance. The figure glanced back over its shoulder, its face hidden by its hood. Quinn pressed himself against the oak-panelled wall to stay out of sight.

The figure turned back to the library doors and slipped inside.

Quinn moved to follow it. Nord's angry voice echoed in his ears: *the library is forbidden to you!* He paused on the threshold, and then decided he had to know. He followed the figure inside.

The library was as dark as a shuttered tomb. In the dim threads of moonlight, Quinn could only just make out the cloaked figure, a blot of solid darkness against the shadowy background of books. It moved back and forth, searching for something.

As he watched, a wizened arm shot out from the cloak. It snatched up a huge, heavy-looking book – the very same one that Quinn had seen before, with the metal clasp.

Quinn took a step forward, risking everything for a better look. The floorboard beneath him gave a loud, traitorous creak.

The figure instantly spun around, the cloak

swirling around it. For the first time, Quinn saw its face. Or what it had *instead* of a face.

Two blank white eyes stared at him out of the black hood, blazing with uncanny light. A swirling screen of fog, like a misty mask, covered the rest of the face. It came swooping at him with an unearthly hiss.

With a yell, Quinn tried to fight it off, but the skinny arms were incredibly strong. The creature slammed into him and knocked him over backwards. Next moment it was on him, heavy and deathly cold as an avalanche.

Quinn struck out blindly. His hands caught and clutched the black cloth of the thing's robe. It hissed in fury and grabbed his wrists, forcing them down, pinning him to the ground.

The horrible blank eyes glared into his. Then a voice began to speak. Quinn couldn't tell if he was hearing it with his ears, or in his mind. It hissed and echoed like some dark thing muttering curses in a vaulted cellar:

'You are not welcome here! Fool. You should have kept your lowly dragon-self hidden!'

It knows who I am. Quinn fought even harder to fling the thing off, but the clawed hands dug into his flesh like thorns, and their grip was like cold metal manacles.

A bluish mist was forming around him, clinging, probing with its icy touch. Whatever this thing was, it was winning. The white eyes glared like twin moons, blotting out everything else with their hypnotic power. Quinn breathed out, shuddering, and a trail of mist came with it, as if the thing was pulling the warm life from his body.

Of course. It was emptying him like an old wineskin, making room for something else. Something ancient, without a body of its own.

Quinn could feel another mind pushing into his, invading his body. The moaning noise was much louder now, roaring like a wind across a mountaintop. It would be so easy just to let go, to let those eyes consume his soul . . .

No! I have to fight this!

With a tremendous effort of will he tore his eyes away. There was only one thing he could do to save his life now and he did it.

Dragonblood blasted through his veins. His spine stretched, bursting out of his back into a lashing tail. He flung his arms forward as they lengthened and long claws speared through his fingertips. The robed thing went flying through the air and crashed into a distant bookcase.

Quinn heaved himself over onto his belly and shook himself. He looked down at his muscular forelimbs, covered with golden scales. The robed thing staggered backwards away from him.

'Gold?' it hissed. 'That's not possible!'

Quinn bared his long teeth. The tide had turned now, and he was on the attack. He lunged at the ethereal figure, which sprang away. Now it was standing with its back to the thin tower window.

'A great dragon,' it said in awed tones. 'Not lowly. But still you shall fall.'

Quinn hesitated for a moment, then let out a roar.

Instead of the jet of flame he'd expected, a blast of icy wind came howling from his jaws. It caught the robed creature full in its blast, sending it tumbling backwards out of the tower window.

It didn't drop; it hung framed by the window like a hovering vampire.

'Blood on the snow!' it hissed. 'We are coming!' Then, squealing like a bat, it flew raggedly away across the snowy wastes.

Quinn lunged after it but could only fit his head and neck through the narrow window. No matter how he heaved, he couldn't cram the bulk of his dragon body through . . . not without pulling the tower wall down around him. All he could do was concentrate on resuming his human form.

Once he was human again, he peered out across the mountain. He looked into the distance, but there was no sign of the figure anywhere in the moonlit snowscape.

Quinn sighed and turned to cross the room again. That was when he noticed the book the figure had been clutching. It had dropped it when it charged at him.

He picked it up, carried it back to the window and by the moonlight he read the title: *Auric Myths and Legends*.

Why did it want this? he wondered. *And why seal a book of myths with a clasp?*

Two words were still ringing in his ears. Words that made no sense to him, but had been spoken in tones of awe.

He whispered them to himself in the silence of the disarray of the library:

'*Great dragon . . .*'

CHAPTER 8

MYTHS AND LEGENDS

The smell of bacon woke Quinn the next morning. He sat up and rubbed his tired eyes, wondering how long he'd slept. It was fully light outside and he could hear voices coming from downstairs. They'd started breakfast without him.

No wonder he'd overslept. With that nightmare he'd had, it was a wonder he'd slept at all. Except . . .

Quinn looked down at his bare arms. There was the deep scratch the eagle had given him, as well as the marks of nails, dug deep into his flesh. That was where the thing had grappled him, before he'd shifted into dragonform and flung it off.

It hadn't been a nightmare. He really had followed that hunched, harsh-voiced creature up to Nord's library. And it had called him a 'great dragon' before flying away across the mountain.

Quinn dressed quickly. He couldn't keep his mind off the fight the night before. Nothing about it made sense. What sort of being had staring, blank white eyes and could fly through the air without wings? Was it some sort of half-demon, or the ghost of a former lord of the White Tower? One thing was for sure: it had the same otherworldly menace as the eagle that had attacked the priest.

Still groggy from sleep, he stumbled down the stairs and pushed his way through into Nord's dining hall. He expected to see Nord glaring at him, demanding to know why he had been in the library without permission, but the throne-like wooden chair at the table's head was empty.

Ignus, Ulric and Thea were sitting waiting for him, halfway through their own breakfasts. Thea gave a casual wave. Across from her a chair skidded out from the table and turned, offering itself for Quinn to sit on.

'Show-off,' he muttered, but he sat in the chair anyway.

'Glad you made it out of bed eventually,' said Ulric. 'We were starting to worry about you. Thea was all for sending up a search party. Coffee?'

'No thanks. Where's Nord?'

'Not here,' said Ignus.

'I can see that. So where *is* he?'

Thea shrugged. 'Your guess is as good as ours.'

Quinn gave up. This morning was already proving way too complicated. Food was something he could get to grips with. He helped himself to toast, butter, pancakes and a huge scoop of faeberry preserve that melted across his plate in a glossy blue lake.

De Witt entered carrying a tall silver pot of coffee for Ulric. 'Ah,' he said, eyeing Quinn. 'I see your companion has risen from the dead at last.'

'Joyful news,' said Ulric over a mouthful of bacon.

De Witt set the coffee down and peered closely at Quinn. 'I'm sure it's not my place to say so, young man, but you do look very tired. Are you not sleeping well?'

Quinn locked eyes with the butler. 'I'm sleeping just fine, thanks.'

'Indeed? Well, I hope you're not a sleepwalker. Imagine roaming around at night in a tower like this, with all our steep stairs and high balconies. It could be fatal.'

'I bet.'

'Perhaps I could have a word with the head cook? She could make you a hot milky beverage. You'll sleep like a baby then.'

That would suit you down to the ground, wouldn't it, you creepy weirdo. Quinn glared at the man. 'I said, everything's fine, and we are leaving today in any case!'

With a dismissive sniff, De Witt set about

pouring coffee and cleaning away the dirty breakfast plates.

Quinn sat eating, feeling uncomfortable, as the two Dragon Knights and Thea looked suspiciously at him.

'Anything you'd like to share?' Thea offered.

Quinn gave her a warning glance and jerked his head towards De Witt, hoping she'd get the message. He wasn't going to say anything in front of him.

Thea made a silent O with her lips and gave an almost unnoticeable nod. Quinn was glad he could count on her.

'So, Master De Witt,' Thea said brightly, 'where's Nord taken himself off to this merry morning?'

De Witt gave her a level gaze and raised an eyebrow. 'He is indisposed.'

'Oh? Why?'

'Let's say this particular morning is not so "merry" for him,' De Witt said.

Ignus let out a sigh. 'Of course. He's remembering *her*, isn't he?'

De Witt hesitated, then nodded. 'I should not be telling you this, but today is the Lady Catherine's birthday. Once, it was the happiest day of Nord's year. Now it is the saddest.' The butler whisked away Quinn's plate, although he hadn't finished eating, and ignored Quinn's angry scowl.

'Ordinarily, Nord would retire to the library and spend the day reading poetry alone,' De Witt continued, 'since it was Lady Catherine's favourite room in the whole White Tower. But since the pair of you so carelessly *desecrated* her library, he cannot stand to be in the tower at all today, and so he has gone to get some fresh air.'

'Where?' Quinn demanded.

De Witt was silent for a long time, then said, 'If you were truly determined to seek him out, you would find him at the Winter Eyrie. But for your sake, young man, I hope you are not that rude. You have sorely tried his patience already.'

While Ignus and Ulric left to practise jousting in the courtyard, Quinn and Thea found somewhere to talk, privately. Grabbing the copy of *Auric Myths and Legends* from under his bed when the servants weren't looking, they headed to a balcony halfway up the tower. The balcony was half obscured behind doors of pale blue and citrine glass, with seats so guests could look at the view of the mountains. It was as private as they were going to get.

They made themselves comfortable and Quinn filled Thea in on the strange goings-on the previous night.

'The thing that attacked you had white eyes, you say?' she asked.

Quinn nodded. 'Just like Morton's when he had that really bad attack of mountain chill.'

'Ha!' said Thea. 'You want to know what's really going on in a rich man's house? Ask the servants. I sneaked down to the kitchens and listened in. You know what mountain chill *really* is?'

'Tell me.'

'It's just a cold, with a light fever! Whatever Morton has is something pretty serious. They're just calling it mountain chill so we won't ask questions. And he's not the only person to have it, either. People in the town have gone down with the same thing.'

Quinn remembered the icy feel of the creature's skin, and how freezing winds had seemed to blow through his skull when it had stared at him. Gooseflesh rose on his arm at the memory. He shuddered and passed Thea the book.

'So this is the book the creature was after?' Thea asked. 'We've got to look inside!'

'Wait. There's one more thing,' said Quinn. 'When it saw my gold scales, it seemed surprised. It called me a great dragon.'

'Probably just paying you a compliment,' Thea said.

'But why . . .?' Quinn tried to say, although Thea seemed much more interested in getting the book open. She prised the stiff clasp apart and laid the book open on her lap with a satisfied sigh.

The parchment of the pages was golden-yellow, the lettering crisp and black with flourishes of metallic blue and red. It was some strange, thorn-like alphabet Quinn had never seen before. Thea gingerly ran a finger down a column of writing.

'Can you read this?' she asked.

'No. You?'

'Never seen anything like it before. It might be ancient Sethurian, or a dialect of Cantish . . . Let's see if it's all like this.'

Fortunately, some sections of the book were in standard script. Thea excitedly leafed through them until she found an illustration of two blazing white eyes staring out of a misty fog.

'That's it! The thing I saw last night!' Quinn said excitedly. 'White eyes in a mask made from mist.'

'Listen to this. "In a time before time,"' Thea read, '"malevolent spirits inhabited the mountains. They were formed not of flesh, but of wind and snow and magic. Some say they were the evil dreams of a sleeping ice titan who was trapped in a glacier many centuries before the coming of mankind; they drifted forth from his skull and took on bodies of mist."'

'So what happened to them?'

Thea pointed to an illustration of the half-built Auric Citadel. "'When men came and covered the mountaintop with their quarried stones and their babbling voices, the spirits were dismayed. For men brought light and heat and song around the hearth-fires. All these things did the spirits despise. They retreated from the lonely peak where they had dwelled for so long and left the humans in spiteful isolation.'"

From somewhere off in the distance came the scream of an eagle. Thea started, gave Quinn a look and carried on reading:

"'Yet, it is said that the spirits still dwell in the dark spaces between the clouds and the snow, dancing on the winds. Some believe they hate mankind to this very day, and visit mischief upon them. The folk of the Auric Citadel tell strange tales of uncanny illnesses, wherein the very breath of life becomes cold as winter fog. It is even whispered that the spirits . . ."'

Thea stopped reading and gasped out loud. Quinn looked at the passage she was pointing to.

It is even whispered that the spirits may drive a mortal soul out of the body, and claim that body for themselves, dwelling in it as a thief dwells in another's house. And those who are claimed thus become like unto the living dead, be they beast or man.

Quinn and Thea looked at each other in alarm.

'"Be they beast or man!"' Quinn repeated. 'That explains the eagle in the marketplace. The priest must have meant the eagle was possessed by a mountain spirit.'

'Not just the eagle,' Thea said, and swallowed. 'You know, Quinn . . . back when I said I thought poor old Morton had something worse than mountain chill? I think we just found out what it is . . . and it's a *lot* worse.' She pointed to the picture of the raging ice spirit.

Quinn leapt to his feet. 'You and I need to go and check on Morton. Right now.'

CHAPTER 9

THE WINTER EYRIE

Quinn and Thea shoved their way through the glass doors and back inside the tower. They ran down the corridor until Thea found a maidservant dusting the ornaments.

'Where's Morton?' she asked the girl. 'We need to find him. It's urgent.'

The maid rolled her eyes. 'He's got a whole private room to himself, the lucky thing! Normally he sleeps in the servants' quarters with the rest of us, but the doctor reckons they're too crowded and poor little Morton needs his peace and quiet if he's going to get better. So his lordship's given him one of the guest beds.'

'Great. Where?'

'Next floor up, five doors down on the left.'

Quinn led the way up the tower stairs, already dreading what he would find. The door to Morton's room was standing ajar, and Quinn's heart gave a sick thump in his chest.

'I'm ready,' Thea whispered behind him. 'Let's do it.'

Quinn reached for the doorknob, and hesitated. He wondered if he should rush in, sword in hand, and take anyone who might be lurking there by surprise. Or slip in silently, just in case they had this all wrong . . .

He chose caution. Gently, he pushed the door inwards.

Morton's room was cavernous and dark. A single pale thread of sunlight tracked in from a chink in the curtains, which were blackish-blue velvet, so thick and padded they would have stopped an arrow.

It was stiflingly hot. Quinn guessed the doctor

was trying to drive the 'mountain chill' away with heat, the same way Ignus had. Tapestries hung from the stone walls, smothering the room in heavy cloth.

Quinn moved a little way inside, breathing slow and steady. He could just make out the heaped shape of the bed against the wall, but couldn't tell if Morton was in it.

Are those pillows, or a body? he wondered.

Thea slipped in behind him. He could feel her breath tickling the hairs on the back of his neck. Inside the room, nothing moved.

Suddenly, the door slammed shut, shaking the whole chamber with the thunder of the impact.

With an inhuman groan, Morton sat up in the bed. He didn't move like a normal man. Instead, he levered himself up all at once at the waist, stiffly, like a wooden puppet. Quinn grimaced at the sight.

Morton's head twisted round to face them. The eyes were white ghost-lights, illuminating his haggard face. A white nightgown hung on his body like a burial shroud.

He raised a trembling hand and pointed at Quinn.

'Get thee gone from here,' he said, and his voice was as hollow and soulless as the wind howling around the tower-tops. 'The battle to come is none of thy concern, outlanders.'

'That's not Morton's voice!' Quinn hissed to Thea.

'Nobody's spoken like that in centuries,' Thea answered. 'Whatever's inside Morton's body is old.'

The creature bared its teeth and spoke again: 'The high towers of Auric shall be dashed into the dust. Woe and lamentation shall wrack the warm-blooded. All their tears shall turn to ice!'

'Who are you?' Quinn shouted. 'What did you do to Morton?'

'Morton is *gone*,' grated the thing. 'We are the lost ones, the ancient ones, icicle-fanged, the tearers of warm flesh. Down all the years, we rode the wild wind and screamed our hate to the skies. Now we rally to a new banner.'

'Whose banner?'

The thing angled its head, as if the question amused it, and gave a low chuckle.

'Who do you serve?' Quinn yelled. 'Tell me!'

The creature raised its arms and flew at him in a hissing storm of sheets. Quinn ducked out of its way and a flurry of clawed swipes raked the air above him. It turned, snarling like a wild beast, with mist smoking from its mouth and nose.

'Quinn! Is this what attacked you in the library?' Thea yelled, diving for cover.

'I don't think so. That one had mist covering its face . . .' It was hard to see anything at all in the stuffy gloom. Quinn ducked and dodged as best he could, while the blank-eyed apparition lunged at him. Clearly fighting in the dark suited it just fine.

'You would do well to stand aside, outlander!' Morton levitated high over Quinn's head, then came powering down towards him, screaming like a banshee. Quinn struggled and dropped the copy of *Auric Myths and Legends* as the cold hands locked around his neck.

Thea grabbed a pitcher of water from the

bedside table and smashed it over Morton's head. The creature barely seemed to notice. The water trickled through its hair and froze instantly, forming a crown of jagged ice-spears.

Quinn felt his dragonblood surging within him. He flung Morton away so hard that the young man's body shot up through the air and slammed into the ceiling. Flakes of plaster and ice fell in a shower.

Morton shook himself and kept coming.

How are we meant to stop this thing? Quinn suddenly remembered a passage from the book he'd dropped, about how the mountain spirits hated fire and light . . .

'Thea, the window!'

'Got it!'

Thea launched herself into the air and stayed hovering there. Using her magic to levitate, she flew all the way down the length of the room, over the shattered fragments of pitcher and the torn-up bed, until she reached the heavy velvet curtains. With a single mighty tug, she tore them down.

Sunlight blasted into the room. A shriek ripped through the air. Morton writhed in agony as the light caught him with its full force.

Quinn stared at the gnarled husk of what had once been a young valet. The light revealed Morton for what he had truly become, a skeletal, withered thing like the shrunken mummy of someone who had died long ago out on the barren wastes. Its hands clawed at the air, groping blindly for him.

Now the room was lit, Quinn could see glass vials littering the floor. They were full of murky liquids, some as dark as blood, others transparent like stagnant water. They must have been stolen from the alchemy laboratory; it looked as if someone had been conducting a ghastly experiment.

'You burned me,' gasped the hovering creature. 'Now you will pay.'

'Come at me!' Quinn yelled. He'd had enough. It was time to fight back and fight hard.

He raised his hands and called up his dragon-blood. Once he was in full dragonform, he'd tear the mountain spirit into little pieces. His fingers were already turning to claws.

'Stop!' Thea screamed.

'Huh?' Quinn grunted through a mouthful of suddenly jagged teeth.

'You can't kill him. The real Morton is still in there somewhere!'

Quinn roared with rage. Every drop of his blood was burning with the desire to tear the ice-thing apart, but he knew Thea was right. The thing had lied. Morton wasn't gone. They had to believe he could be brought back.

Quinn reversed the change. As his talons became hands again, he clenched his fists and readied a heavy punch. 'Fine. No killing. I'll just knock him out instead . . .'

Morton flew down as fast as a hawk and body-slammed him, knocking him reeling.

Quinn fought for breath on the floor, rolling back and forth. Glass vials snapped and crunched under him. Morton snatched up the *Auric Legends* book from where it had fallen. He leapt over Quinn, vaulted out of the door and ran down the stairs.

'Gods damn it, he's getting away!' Thea yelled. 'Come on!' She grabbed Quinn's hand and hauled him to his feet. The two of them sprinted down the tower stairs after Morton.

The valet looked back, saw they were still coming and snarled angrily. He knocked a free-standing suit of armour down from its alcove and it fell across their path with a steely crash.

Quinn and Thea jumped over it, landed hard and kept going.

Morton flung his arm out and a blast of wind blew the two front doors wide open. He ran out into the street, with Quinn and Thea sprinting close on his heels.

Their boots pounded on the clean white flag-stones of the Citadel. Morton was getting ahead of them. He weaved in and out of the towns-people in the street with superhuman agility.

They ran and ran until Quinn saw the familiar griffin archway up ahead. Morton was making for the marketplace.

Suddenly, Morton stopped and turned around. He inhaled deeply and breathed out a rolling cloud of thick mist. It flooded into the narrow street, blotting out the shapes of people and even buildings.

Quinn and Thea ran straight into the white fogbank. Quinn could barely see a thing. Through the steamy clouds he could just make out Morton, still in his flapping white night-gown, dash through into a crowd of people and vanish from sight.

By the time the fog had dissipated, Morton was nowhere to be seen. Thea bent over, grip-ping her knees, panting with exhaustion.

'We lost him,' she gasped. 'I can't believe it.'

Quinn looked around at the crowds, trying to see any clue to where Morton might have fled. That was when he noticed how pale many of the citizens looked. They were hunched over, their breath misting in the cold, wheezing and coughing.

'Thea? Tell me I'm imagining this.' He quickly pointed the sick people out to her. Thea gripped his arm as she saw a man glaring at them. His eyes were milky pale, like Morton's had been.

'There are hundreds of them,' Thea whispered.

'They're all sick. What did that book say about strange diseases?'

'The same thing might happen to them that happened to Morton,' Quinn said. 'They've got the same symptoms . . .'

'Morton said Auric would fall! Ignus said nobody could bring an army up here, but Quinn, what if the army's here *already?* All it would take is for all of these people to be possessed!'

Quinn made up his mind. 'We've got to tell Nord what's going on. I don't care whose birthday it is. He's not sitting this one out.'

The merchant Quinn and Ignus had traded with the day before was happy to give him and Thea directions to the Winter Eyrie. He pointed up to the highest part of the Citadel, where the city boundary made way for the sheer rock face of the mountain.

They clambered up a steep stairway, and then had to make their way over unworked rock. Nord was there, perched on an outcrop, looking out over the whole of the Golden Sun island.

He turned to face them as they approached but didn't get up. 'Welcome. There's bread and cold meat in the basket. Help yourselves.'

Quinn stared at the man. He was sitting with his hand on his knee, his long hair blowing in the wind. For some reason, he'd taken the braid out. The anger of the day before seemed to be completely gone, with no sign that it had ever been there, like a clear sky after a storm.

'We need to talk with you,' Quinn said.

Nord nodded. 'And I'd be glad to listen.'

Quinn didn't have time to wonder what had brought about this change. He got straight to the point. 'Your valet, Morton? He doesn't have the "mountain chill". He's possessed by a spirit.'

Nord's face showed no surprise. 'Go on.'

Quinn told him everything they'd learnt. He left nothing out, not even his midnight visit to the library. Thea let him speak, only interrupting to add details he'd left out.

'Someone's planning to destroy your city, and they're going to use the mountain spirits to do it,' Quinn finished.

Nord looked at him with grave, unblinking eyes.

'I know,' he said softly.

'You do?' Thea burst out.

Nord nodded and looked down at the high towers of his beloved city. 'Yes. I've known for a long time. Something has been wrong in Auric for years . . .'

CHAPTER 10

BEFORE THE STORM

Nord gestured for Quinn and Thea to sit beside him.

'Catherine suspected something was amiss long before I did,' he said. 'I take it Ignus has told you about her?'

'A little,' Quinn admitted, 'but not much.'

'We heard she loved the library,' Thea said, with a guilty look.

'She did. She had a passion for old Alarissian folklore. Songs, folk tales, even the rhymes passed down by children playing in the school-yards. She was convinced there were secrets to be unlocked in the old stories. We used to joke about the adventures we'd go on together, once Vayn was defeated. She had me believing in buried tombs full of treasure, lost cities, sunken pirate galleons . . .' Nord sighed at the memory.

'Did she ever find anything like that?' Quinn asked.

'Only once. It was the night before I left for the final battle with Vayn – I remember it clearly. She didn't come down to dinner, so I went to find her to see what was wrong. There she was in the library, bent over an enormous old book of myths. A locked clasp had once held it shut, but she'd picked the lock with one of her hairpins.'

'Girl after my own heart,' said Thea, with a half-smile.

Quinn was busy with his own thoughts. A book of myths held shut with a clasp? It had to be the same one Morton had stolen from him. Now, perhaps, he'd find out what was so special about it.

Nord closed his eyes. 'Catherine was so excited

about what she'd found, she'd forgotten to eat. I couldn't read the script on those pages, but she could. It was a forbidden spell. You know what they are, Thea?'

Thea paled. 'Oh, yes.' She turned to Quinn: 'Forbidden spells are spells so dangerous they have to be magically encrypted in case a junior magician tries to cast them. No wonder I couldn't understand it.'

'Exactly. This was a gate spell, created by Rhotok the Unclean during the Sundering War, centuries ago. If it were ever cast, it would rip open a gate between our world and the spirit world, allowing spirits to enter our realm in vast numbers.'

'Sounds like the kind of book that *needs* a lock on it,' Quinn said. 'But Catherine vanished years ago. What's the book got to do with what's happening now?'

'I'm coming to that,' Nord snapped.

Quinn quickly shut his mouth.

'Catherine discovered that the mountain spirits were more than just myths. They meant us harm, because our ancestors took their home away. But since they were made of magic and mist and had no bodies of their own, they couldn't hurt us like they wanted to.'

'So they have to possess living bodies,' Quinn guessed. 'Like the eagle. And Morton.'

'Yes,' Nord said. For a second, his face showed almost unbearable pain. 'Catherine tried to warn me. I wouldn't listen ... What threat could bodiless spirits be? My head was on fire with thoughts of Vayn and how I must end his evil. So she said that if I could not protect my people, she would.'

Thea whistled. 'Brave of her.'

'Of course she was brave. She was Auric-born!' Nord angrily flung a rock out into space. It bounced and rattled down the mountainside. 'The rest you know ... mostly. Catherine disappeared while I was away fighting Vayn. Ever since, people have been afflicted with the sickness we call "mountain chill" to disguise that of which we speak. Pale eyes, cold skin, speaking in strange voices in the night.'

'But we saw hundreds of people with the sickness,' Quinn said.

'As have I. Normally, we would see three or four a year, at most. The threat is escalating, and there is magic behind it. Magic not of this world.' Nord stood and began to walk away, then turned back to them. 'Now do you see why I cannot leave the Auric Citadel?'

The afternoon of the Blood Moon festival saw Quinn practising his archery in the courtyard while Ignus looked on. Now that Nord had opened up to him and Thea, all talk of leaving the White Tower had ceased.

'You did know Nord was a champion archer when you challenged him, right?' Ignus passed Quinn a fresh fistful of arrows.

'Of course I knew!' Quinn notched an arrow. There was a routine to shooting well, he'd learnt. Breathe in on the pull, hold, and breathe out as you loose.

'So how in the gods' names do you expect to win?'

Quinn hauled the bowstring back, breathing in. Next came the magic moment, the aim. If you thought about it too much, your hand would tremble and the shot would miss the mark. But if you just fired without thinking at all, trusting to instinct alone, you might as well roll dice to get a result. The art of the perfect shot lay in not *trying* to be perfect. It was a riddle, a paradox.

He loosed the arrow. It thwacked into the target just above the gold centre.

'I don't expect to win,' Quinn said.

'Then why are you even trying?'

'Because I have to, Ignus. If I don't try, I don't have any chance at all. Even the smallest chance is better than none.'

Ignus grunted, apparently satisfied.

Quinn was glad the big man had stayed to help him practise while Ulric and Nord set off to the town square. As one of the local lords, Nord had a duty to prepare for the festival, and Ulric was only too glad to help him.

Quinn readied his next shot. He was getting

better. Even Ignus could see that. Maybe his dragonblood was helping him learn faster than ordinary humans. *Who knows?* he thought. *Maybe I'll win the archery contest after all.*

Even if he did, would Nord keep his promise? After his words the day before, it didn't seem likely, even if he had once been an honourable Dragon Knight. Nord saw himself as the protector of Auric, just as his ancestors had been. While the mountain spirits were still a threat, Nord would be compelled to stay here.

Almost as if someone wanted it that way . . .

Trying to get to the bottom of this was like groping your way through thick fog. They had to pierce it and find the truth.

In one fluid move, Quinn notched, drew back and shot his arrow. It flew straight as a sunray and slammed into the gold. The shaft went in so deep that the feathers met the straw.

'Excellent!' Ignus laughed. 'Here. You have a rest. Let me have a go.'

Ignus took the bow, notched an arrow and drew back the bowstring. His nostrils flared and his cheeks puffed out. Quinn tried not to laugh.

Ignus fired – and the arrow zipped halfway to the target before stopping in mid-air. It hung there, unmoving.

'What?' Ignus bellowed.

The arrow suddenly dropped to the ground with a clatter.

Laughing, Thea stepped out from behind a statue. She wiggled her fingers in front of her face. 'Sorry, Ignus. Couldn't resist a spot of magic.'

'Can't you find something useful to do?' Ignus grumbled.

'I have!' Thea vaulted into a chair and sat straddling the back. 'While you two have been shooting arrows into poor helpless targets, I've been in the library.'

'The library?' Quinn spluttered. 'Nord will kill you if he finds out!'

'So don't tell him. Now listen. This is important. It's about the mountain spirits.'

Carefully, she drew out a rolled-up length of parchment and opened it up for them to see.

'One of Nord's ancestors wrote this. It's all about the spirits and what they can do . . . and can't do, more importantly. He talks about the powers they get when they take over a human body. Flight, great strength, that sort of thing.'

'Which we knew about already,' Quinn said.

'Right. But here's what we didn't know. They can't just possess people without help. The host body has to be *defiled* first, either with dark magic or some other means.'

Ignus raised an eyebrow. 'Defiled?'

'Corrupted, made unclean. Only a few creatures in all of history have that kind of power. One of them is Warathu, the queen of the mountain spirits. Another is Vayn.'

Quinn slowly nodded. The picture was coming together at last. This had Vayn's fingerprints all over it.

Thea took a deep breath before speaking again. 'The spirit you fought in the library that night? I think that was Warathu herself.'

'The queen?'

'Yes. She's been spreading the magical corruption

that we thought was an illness, to prepare host bodies for her fellow spirits!'

Ignus groaned. 'Of course. It makes sense. "Mountain chill" indeed!'

'So if we destroy the queen spirit, it'll end the corruption?' Quinn said excitedly.

'I think so,' said Thea. 'Almost all magic dies when its creator dies. The trick is going to be finding Warathu. We don't know whose body she's hiding in.'

Quinn fingered the hilt of his sword. 'Oh, I think we do.' He leapt out of his chair and began to pace back and forth. 'Who was creeping about on the night I got attacked? Who's been threatening me ever since we came? He's been here for years – knows the tower inside out – hell, he probably killed Catherine and got rid of her body somewhere!' He looked at Ignus and Thea's blank faces. 'What, do I have to spell it out? It's De Witt!'

Ignus and Thea looked at one another.

'Agreed,' said Thea, and Ignus nodded too.

'Never did like the man,' he added. 'Weaselly little so-and-so.'

'We have to warn Nord. Now.'

'Wait. One more thing,' said Thea. 'Nord's ancestor says the spirits are a part of nature, and that means they can use the power of major natural events to boost their own.'

Quinn felt a chill. 'Like a Blood Moon eclipse, you mean?'

'You've got it. Whatever hell Warathu is planning to unleash, it's coming *today*. In just under three hours . . .'

CHAPTER II

THE CONTEST

'Nord's in charge of the Blood Moon festival. Whatever's coming through, he'll be right in its path,' Quinn said. 'We need to warn him, and fast.'

'Wait! This is something we can settle ourselves! Let's search the tower for De Witt, and when we find him, we deal with him.' Ignus slammed a meaty fist into his open palm.

'No,' Quinn said.

Ignus bristled. 'No? And why not, Your *Majesty*?'

'Because De Witt is cleverer than that, of

course! He won't be lurking in the White Tower. He'll have gone with Nord, so he can meet up with Morton in secret. What's more natural than a servant accompanying his master to the festival?'

'He's got a point,' Thea admitted. 'Let's go.'

Night was stealing across the Citadel as Quinn, Thea and Ignus rushed through the streets. There wasn't a soul in sight to bar their way. Even the guards in the doorways and street corners were missing.

'Probably given the night off,' Thea gasped. 'Everyone in Auric's going to be at the festival. To soak up the good luck that radiates from the Blood Moon.'

'There won't be much good luck going around if Warathu has her way,' Quinn replied.

Ignus led them to the grand public courtyard in the south side of Auric. It lay in front of a huge mausoleum-like building with wide steps, which housed the town hall and law court. On the rooftops and turrets, spires tipped with iron lances jetted forth flame into the darkening sky, lighting up the whole square. It reminded Quinn of dragon breath.

'It's an alchemical reaction,' Thea said, as if she'd read his mind.

The courtyard was packed with a heaving mass of people. They were pressing up against a fenced-off area in front of the town hall, all ready for the festival.

Several wooden thrones had been set up at the top of the town-hall steps, turning them into a marble podium. From overhead the banners of the seven noble families of Auric fluttered in the breeze, resplendent in bright colours. Nord's banner held the central place of honour.

Quinn glimpsed the tips of lances waving above people's heads and heard the neighing of horses: *So, the jousting has begun*, he thought.

'We need to get to the front!' he called.

'Say no more,' said Ignus. 'Pardon me! Coming through!'

Ignoring the angry yells and rude words flung his way, the big man barged through the crowd like a bull through a field of thistles. Quinn and

Thea hurried along in his wake until they were right up against the rope fence.

Armoured contestants were riding horses at one another down a long strip of grass. Lances shattered against shields. Sometimes a rider would be knocked clean off his seat to land with a jangling crash on the hard ground. The lucky ones were able to stagger off the field themselves, but most had to be carried off by long-suffering servants.

Quinn looked to the left and right, searching the crowd for any glimpse of De Witt.

'See him, Thea?'

'No. Ignus?'

'Little weasel's hiding somewhere,' grunted Ignus. 'Can't you cast a traitor-finding spell, Thea?'

'Wish I could,' Thea sighed.

'It's Ulric we need,' said Quinn. 'He can use his shadow magic to disguise himself. That way, he can search this crowd without being noticed.'

Thea grinned. 'Good thinking! De Witt and Morton are going to be looking out for us, and Ulric can trick them . . . Where *is* Ulric, anyway?'

Ignus pointed at the jousting field. 'Where Ulric always is. Tricking someone.'

Ulric had entered the jousting, and he was one of the two riders competing right in front of them. Quinn recognised the Dragon Knight's helmet.

Clearly old habits died hard, because Ulric was cheating. Every time he rode against his opponent, the rider opposite aimed his lance squarely at Ulric, only for it to miss completely. Quinn saw a flicker of shadow magic every time it happened.

Eventually, Ulric unhorsed the man, to the accompaniment of cheers.

'I must have hit my head in practice,' complained his opponent as he was led off the field. 'He kept going all blurry.'

Ulric swaggered over to the excited crowd and waved, making them cheer even harder.

'Ulric!' Quinn yelled over the noise. '*Ulric!*'

Ulric either couldn't hear him or didn't want to. Quinn kept shouting his name again and again until eventually Ulric casually wandered over.

He said through a fixed grin: 'Don't blow this for me, laddie, and there's a gold coin in it for you afterwards. Deal?'

'There are more important things to worry about right now,' Quinn seethed, 'and better uses for shadow magic than cheating in jousting contests! We need to find De Witt. I'm ordering you to find him. Use shadow magic if you need to. Understand?'

Ulric was suddenly a lot more serious. 'Yes, of course, Your Majesty. I'll find him.'

Before Quinn could do anything else, a call came from a white-haired figure at the top of the steps. 'We will now proceed to the archery contest.' The man fumbled with a scroll of names. 'It appears there is, uh, only one challenger this year . . .'

Nord's voice rang out clear and loud, interrupting. 'Quinn! Are you here?' He put his hands on his hips and surveyed the crowd. 'You're not going to keep me waiting, are you?'

Laughter rippled through the crowd.

Quinn stood, dismayed. So the contest was

going to be a head-to-head? It made sense, he supposed. Nobody else would dare pit their skills against Nord's. Nobody else was foolish enough.

'I see him!' Nord roared, and pointed right at Quinn.

'Stop!' Quinn protested. 'There's no time for this! We need to find . . . *oof!*' A burly man had shoved him forward.

'What are you waiting for? Go and compete, boy!' the man said heartily. 'Don't get cold feet now you've come this far.'

'That's right! Bad luck to back out of a contest, today of all days!' said an old woman beside him.

The crowd began to push him forward. No matter what Quinn tried to say, a hundred hands seemed to shove and jostle him on. Someone lifted the rope barrier, and suddenly Quinn found himself standing in the open festival space, with the crowd cheering him. There was no way back. He couldn't even see Ignus and Thea any more.

Nord swept down the steps, smiling, and patted Quinn on the shoulder. 'For a moment there, I thought you'd lost your nerve. Come. Let us begin.'

'You have to listen,' Quinn burst out. 'That danger threatening Auric? We know what it is, and we know *who* it is . . .'

But Nord was already walking back across the festival ground. Quinn's words were lost in the roar of the crowd.

There was nothing for it but to follow.

Labourers were busily taking down the rail that had run the length of the jousting field and dragging two straw targets into place in front of the town-hall steps. Quinn noticed four or five unused targets standing huddled at the edge of the field, and cursed his luck for being Nord's only challenger.

The Master of Ceremonies drew a chalk line where they were to stand. As Nord and Quinn took their places, Quinn hissed, 'I need to talk to you.'

'Very well. The competition will have to wait.'

Nord tried to lead Quinn away, but a roar went up from the crowds. A few people crawled under the rope barrier and ran towards Quinn, yelling furiously:

'You'll anger the gods!'

'Come on, your lordship!'

'It's almost Blood Moon!'

As the guards ran forward to drag the protestors back, Nord gave Quinn an apologetic look. Quinn clenched his jaw in frustration and headed back to the chalk line.

Nord accepted his bow from the pageboy, who held one out to Quinn as well. The crowd roared again as he took it, this time with approval. He felt angry, sick and fighting-mad all at once, as if he was trapped on a runaway chariot.

'This shall be a test of skill before the gods,' wheezed the Master of Ceremonies. 'Ten arrows each. Whoever scores the highest shall be named champion. By ancient accord, any man whose shot draws blood shall be disqualified.'

Quinn wondered what ancient accident – or worse – had led to *that* rule of the contest. 'I'll try not to kill anyone,' he muttered as he accepted the offered quiver of arrows.

'Come, come. You're not *that* hopeless,' Nord said with a tight smile.

The Master of Ceremonies blew on a gigantic horn to start the contest. Nord and Quinn notched their first arrows.

Quinn steadied himself, controlled his breathing and shot. *Thunk.* A gold, but only just; it was kissing the circle's edge.

Thunk. Nord's shot went straight to the heart of the gold as if it belonged there. Fresh cheering broke out.

'The queen of the mountain spirits has possessed De Witt,' Quinn said as Nord reached for his second arrow.

'Are you trying to put me off by making me laugh?' Nord said coolly.

They shot again. A respectable blue for Quinn, while Nord notched up his second gold. Now Quinn was trailing.

'You have to listen!' Quinn insisted. 'The whole Citadel is in danger. It's not even De Witt's fault . . . he's possessed.'

Nord shook his head. 'De Witt conspire

against me? Impossible. I know he can be difficult, but he has served me loyally for years.
Shoot, damn you.'

'Possessed by Warathu herself!'

That made Nord stop and stare. 'Warathu?
Dear gods. Catherine mentioned that name . . .'

'SHOOT!' roared the crowd.

Their third and fourth shots told the same
sorry tale as before. Quinn's words had rattled
Nord's concentration, however. On his fifth shot
Nord planted an arrow in the outermost black
ring, making the crowd gasp.

That brought the scores closer, but Nord was
still way out in front. Quinn glanced at the
unused group of spare targets again, wishing he
didn't have to compete like this in front of
everyone.

Then he froze. A figure in a black cloak was
standing, motionless, among the targets. Even
at this distance, he was sure it was the one who'd
attacked him in the library.

'Nord, it's Warathu,' he said. 'Here, now.
Look!'

'We have to abandon the contest,' Nord said. 'Blood Moon or not, the Citadel needs protection.'

He put down his bow. The yells of outrage from the crowd were deafening. The Master of Ceremonies was shaking his head sternly. He pointed at Quinn; it was his turn to shoot.

I have to finish this, Quinn thought, *or that crowd will tear me to bits*. With shaking hands, he notched, drew and fired. The arrow went completely wild. It shot past the target and shattered against the marble steps beyond. Someone in the crowd booed, but to Quinn's immense gratitude, nobody else joined in.

He looked back at the targets. The cloaked figure was gone.

The remaining bowshots passed in a blur. Quinn just wanted to get it over with. It wasn't long before he heard cheering and shouts and realised the contest had ended. Nord had won, just like everyone had expected.

Nord offered Quinn his hand to shake. 'Well done. Now let's get out of here and find Warathu.'

'De Witt might have slipped into the crowd,'

Quinn guessed. 'Let's go and look . . .' The Master of Ceremonies hurried over to them. 'Wait. You cannot leave. The festival is not over!'

Nord bared his teeth. 'Damn it, Quinn, he's right. They have to present the medals.'

'Fine. I'll go and look for De Witt, since I lost.'

'No. I may have won the gold medal, but the silver goes to you. You have to sit with me in the champions' place of honour.'

Quinn had no choice but to follow as Nord strode up the steps to the row of wooden thrones. Other champions from the day's competitions were sitting there already: a warrior in armour, a scarred girl with a rapier at her belt and a man wearing only a loincloth, covered with claw marks. One of the thrones was empty: Ulric's.

'You may have lost the wager,' Nord said quietly, 'but if my people are truly in danger, then I will fight by your side to protect them.'

The moon had risen from behind the White Tower, and was almost directly overhead now.

From somewhere, unseen trumpets blew a fanfare. A stooped figure in a red-and-gold robe slowly approached them. A priest, Quinn saw.

'Blessings be upon the champions of Auric, on this day of the Blood Moon!' the priest chanted. Quinn realised it was the same man he'd saved from the possessed eagle in the marketplace.

The priest came closer and wafted incense at them. He caught Quinn's eye and smiled. 'I owe you my life, young man. Once again, thank you.'

'You're welcome,' Quinn told him.

The priest leaned close and whispered, 'There is a plague in this city, my friend. The mountain spirits are behind it. Did you know?'

'Yes,' Quinn whispered. 'We're trying to stop them.'

The priest nodded, then frowned. 'So strange. People have many different illnesses, and yet they all develop into the white-eye plague.'

Quinn sat bolt upright. 'What did you say?'

'One has a cough, another a cold, a third a fever. And yet within days, all three have the spirit sickness. It is almost as if seeing the doctor makes it worse.'

The priest moved on, chanting and leaving a trail of incense behind him.

A gong struck. Overhead, a red blush began to spread across the moon.

Quinn sat with the priest's words echoing in his mind. They had made him deeply uneasy. All at once he had a terrifying thought:

What if De Witt wasn't behind this after all?

CHAPTER 12

BLOOD MOON

'The Blood Moon is upon us!' cried the priest.

Quinn looked up. The full moon was directly over the Citadel. In a single instant the lunar disc changed from pale, calm silver to glaring red, as if the eye of a mad god had suddenly opened.

The whole Citadel was drenched in red light. The crowd cooed in awe at the spectacle. People laughed at how uncanny they suddenly looked to one another. Hands and faces shone crimson. Between one moment and the next, a town square full of people had become a demons' masquerade.

'Good fortune be with us all,' the priest declared. 'Let the gods see the best of us duly rewarded. Present the medals.'

The Master of Ceremonies came forward with Nord's golden medal on a cushion. Quinn sat, every muscle tense, gripping the arms of his chair. Something terrible was about to happen. He knew it in the marrow of his bones.

'For skill in archery,' announced the Master of Ceremonies, 'I present you with –'

As if on cue, a shrill cackle cut him off in mid-sentence.

From the shadows, a black-cloaked figure came rushing like a spectre, arms outstretched. It flung the Master of Ceremonies aside as if he were a rag doll and raised its skinny arms into the full glare of the Blood Moon. Nord and Quinn sprang from their chairs at once.

The figure threw back its hood. Quinn saw the blazing eyes and the mask of swirling mist, just as he had in the library. As the mist-mask faded away, revealing a face, he saw – too late – just how wrong he had been.

It was not De Witt whom Warathu had possessed, but the white-haired old doctor, Margery Devereux. There was no kindliness in her expression now. The aged face was twisted with hate.

She snapped her fingers. 'Morton? To me, boy!'

Morton came running out of the darkness, loping on all fours as if he were a dog. Like hers, his face was a crooked mockery of what it had once been. The mountain spirit in him was deforming his flesh, making him hideous, barely recognisable.

Screams rang out from the crowd. Frantic people fought to get away, but there were too many of them packed into one place.

The doctor threw back her head and let loose a volley of foul laughter. 'Pitiful, soft man-children! Did you think you were safe, snug in your high mountain? Did you trust in walls to protect you?' She snarled. 'Fools. There is nowhere to hide from Emperor Vayn in all of Alariss. His anger is great. And it is turned upon you!'

As the townspeople tried to flee, Quinn drew his sword.

'Warathu!' he yelled. 'I know who you are, spirit. You've been making the people sick – you created the plague!'

The doctor craned her head round to glare at him, and the bones of her neck made a ghastly cracking noise as she moved. 'Oh, yes. Plenty of human fools have been corrupted. My experiments have been most fruitful.' She patted Morton on the head. 'The vessels are ready. It is time to fill them.'

Nord drew back his bow and took aim at her head. 'Not in *my* city!'

The doctor flung her hand out and a spear of ice shot through the air, heading straight for Nord. He dived out of the way. The ice-spear shattered, showering Nord and Quinn with freezing fragments.

'The time when you could have stopped me has long passed,' gloated the doctor. 'Through the power of the Blood Moon, a new army of spirit warriors will be created. First, we shall tear down your city, then we shall fly to our new master, Emperor Vayn. Vengeance has been long in coming!'

A halo of red light like a fiery crown shone out from the Blood Moon. The doctor opened the *Auric Myths and Legends* book and began to chant.

'The gate spell,' Nord said in horror. 'She's calling her brethren through.'

The air around the doctor seemed to seethe and boil, as if reality itself were being melted and malformed. Scarlet light leapt from the book, forming into shimmering runes and dancing in a perfect circle. The doctor's eyes shone blindingly bright with the force of her magic. She dropped the book, stretched her arms out wide and let out a cry of agonised triumph.

Next second, energy exploded from her hands and face. The ghostly forms of mountain spirits came roaring through the ring of runes, funnelling into the real world. Quinn watched it all unfold before him like a bystander at a horrific accident. It seemed there was nothing he could do.

The mountain spirits rushed through the air in torrents, like malevolent water-serpents borne along in a powerful river, and fountained out across the screaming crowd.

Quinn saw a spirit lunge towards one of the plague victims, a woman who was almost doubled over from the illness. Her body jerked as the spirit took possession of her. Evil strength poured into her body. She stood upright, her eyes shining with cold light, grinning like a skeleton.

'Merciful gods,' gasped the priest. 'There are so many of them!'

Quinn saw what he meant. Hundreds of spirits were latching on to the sickly citizens and forcing themselves into their weakened bodies. The remaining townsfolk were flooding out of the square, trampling over one another as they ran for their lives. Even the city guards, all but a brave few, were running away.

He heard a familiar voice shout: 'This way! We'll keep them off you!' It was Ignus, standing side by side with Ulric and Thea. Along with a handful of Auric guards, the three of them were defending the main street that led out of the town square.

As the flood of screaming citizens rushed through, desperate to find safety, some of the possessed ones rose up into the air and came after them. They hurled ice-spears, like the one the doctor had conjured. The citizens they struck froze on the spot, clamped to the ground with welts of ice.

Ignus and Ulric shifted into dragonform. They fought back against the spirits, lashing out with claws and tail swipes.

'Pull your blows!' Ignus roared. 'Strike to subdue, not to kill!'

Quinn understood. *The spirits might be evil, but the people they're possessing aren't. The Dragon Knights can't risk hurting innocent people. But how else are we going to stop Warathu?*

'If we take the queen spirit down, we'll banish all the others!' Quinn yelled to Nord.

Nord looked grim. 'The doctor may die. Very

well. If any of us must shed innocent blood, let it be me. Stay back!'

'I won't let you do this alone.'

'You must!'

Nord gestured, and a blast of wind knocked Quinn off his feet. He flew back and crashed into one of the stone pillars fronting the town hall.

Groggy, through blurred eyes, he saw Nord confront the doctor. Nord loosed arrow after arrow, each one streaking forth with the force of a storm-wind. Not a single one even came close. The doctor shrieked with high, crazed laughter as she smashed Nord's arrows out of the air with windblasts of her own.

It was storm against storm. But with Vayn's manacle binding him, Nord's powers were weak. The doctor swept her arms upwards as if she were gathering up a bundle, and a violent blast of wind flung Nord up into the air. He fell from the height of a rooftop and struck the flagstones hard.

Nord lay gasping and beaten, with blood flowing from his nose, as the queen of the wind spirits loomed over him . . .

CHAPTER 13

SPIRIT QUEEN

'First the lord falls, then the city,' jeered the doctor. 'Today your proud bloodline ends!' She grasped Nord's shirtfront and raised a hand, ready to strike the killing blow.

Quinn ran forward and leapt into the air. Wings burst from his back. Beating hard, they held him aloft while his body morphed and changed. It took him only seconds to complete the transformation.

The doctor slowly looked up at him and snarled. 'Great dragon. Again you vex me. You dare stand between Warathu and her rightful prey?'

Quinn faced her and roared out his challenge. She spread her clawed fingers. He knew she meant to tear Nord's throat out.

There was no time for clever strategies. Brute force would have to do. Quinn lowered his head and flew right at the doctor, as fast as he could.

He caught her body on his scaly shoulder and bore her with him through the air. With no room to turn and no way to stop, they crashed into the wall in front of them – and through it.

Quinn lay dazed in the hole he'd smashed through the town-hall wall. Broken marble blocks lay scattered everywhere. Trickles of stone dust rained down on him. He pulled himself backwards, using all four legs, trying to get free before any more of the wall collapsed.

The doctor lay exposed, flat on her back among the debris. She struggled and sat up, just as Quinn pulled his body back out of the hole. Something gave way. A fresh shower of rubble came down, burying the doctor completely.

Is she dead? he wondered.

He couldn't tell. But the mountain spirits were still rushing through the gate she'd opened, so either Thea had been wrong about killing the queen, or she was still alive under that heap of masonry.

'Quinn!' gasped a voice behind him. 'Your Majesty . . .'

Nord! Quinn hastily resumed his human form and ran over to where Nord lay groaning.

'I was wrong,' Nord said. 'I should have joined you from the start. You have been brave and honest, and I have been a blind fool.' Wincing in pain, he pulled himself up into a kneeling position. 'Will you knight me now?'

Quinn drew his father's sword. Golden light blazed from it. He brought the blade down on Nord's shoulder. The familiar words burst from his mouth in the ancient Draconic tongue:

'By the power of dragonblood and in the sight of the gods, I bind you to protect the Twelve Islands against all threat and I bind your loyalty to the true Emperor. Advance, Nord, Dragon Knight of the Twelve Islands.'

With a juddering crack like the sound of lightning, the manacle shattered.

Fresh strength poured into Nord's body. He stood and closed his eyes. They flicked open again, revealing churning ice-blue lenses: *dragon eyes.*

No two Dragon Knights changed form in exactly the same way. Nord's whole body rippled like a cracking whip. Next moment, a silver-blue dragon stood where he had been, leaner than the other dragons and with a white crest that shone like moonlight.

Most of the townsfolk had fled the central square now, but the spirits were still rushing through from the otherworld and hurtling off through the city, hunting for sick citizens to possess.

'Nord, we have to close the gate!' Quinn shouted.

'Leave it to me.' Nord's dragon-voice was deep and haunting, like the wind through the pine forests. He flew up above the town square and began to fly in a tight circle, making a whirling vortex of silver-blue.

This was true storm magic. Dark clouds gathered overhead, swelling and thickening like ink spilled into water, with quick pulses of electricity lighting them up from within. Quinn watched in awe as the Dragon Knight filled up the sky with heavy thunderheads.

The clouds grew until they blotted out the Blood Moon completely.

Now that the red rays no longer shone, there was no power to hold Warathu's gate open. The dancing runes faded and the spell faltered and died.

Quinn shifted back into dragonform and flew up to join Nord in the sky. Possessed citizens were chasing wildly through the city streets now, letting rip with windblasts and ice-javelins, laughing at the chaos.

'How do we stop the possessed ones without hurting them?' Quinn said.

'Like this!' Nord told him. He beat his wings and shot forward, heading towards a possessed merchant. The man was hovering by a tower window, with icy mist curling from his hair. Two children inside the tower begged and pleaded with him to leave them alone.

Nord breathed a blast of freezing air. The man stiffened and made choking, gasping noises. A crust of ice formed on his body. He slowly dropped from the sky and toppled over in the street, lying still as a marble statue, only his eyes moving in his skull.

'I've heard of fighting fire with fire, but never ice with ice!' Quinn said.

A memory flashed upon him. In the library, he'd instinctively breathed ice at Warathu. He had the same power as Nord. They could contain the spirit outbreak together!

Nord and Quinn flew along the torchlit streets of the Citadel, hunting down the possessed citizens and freezing them one by one. The spirits fought back, battering at the dragons with weather magic of their own. Once, Quinn cornered three spirits in a blind alley and was about to freeze them all with one blast, only for the spirits to attack with a combined windstorm that smashed Quinn against a cliff side and nearly snapped the bones in his right wing. Nord swept in and breathed on the trio until they were three unrecognisable mounds of ice.

'Thanks,' Quinn gasped, shaking rock fragments off his long body. 'You're *sure* our ice breath isn't hurting the possessed people?'

'I would never hurt my own citizens,' Nord said. 'The spirits within them protect them from the cold, so the ice merely holds them immobile . . . Quinn, look out!'

An angry shriek told them that Margery Devereux had dug her way out of the rubble. She twisted her hands around in magical gestures. A sudden choking feeling seized Quinn's throat, as if clawed hands were strangling him.

'You shall breathe no more, great dragon,' she said, her words dripping with hate.

Quinn struggled. His dragonform writhed and jerked in the air like a mighty sea serpent caught on a ship's anchor chain. Summoning all his strength, he spun around in a full mid-air somersault and brought his tail down in a power slam.

The doctor yelled and dived out of the way, her spell broken.

Quinn's tail split the town-hall steps in half, showering the area with fragments of masonry.

As the doctor coughed and tried to ready another attack, a barrage of stone missiles thudded into her body and knocked her sideways in a long skid.

Thea stood on the lowest step, her hands raised, her fingers crackling with raw magic.

'You threaten me?' hissed the doctor. 'What do you know of magic? You are a mere stripling child.'

Thea cocked her head. 'You have to watch out for the young ones. We'll always surprise you.'

She quickly gestured, a twist-and-punch that sent a fresh volley of stones whistling through the air. They pummelled the spot where the doctor stood, blotting her out of sight. Quinn could just make out a single clawed hand that waved feebly through the choking dust.

'We've got her on the back foot!' Thea yelled. 'Quinn, take her down!'

'No!' wailed the doctor. She burst through the dust clouds, flew over the town square like a shrieking harpy and vanished behind the roof-tops. Beyond, the golden dome of the White Tower could be seen gleaming through the night.

'Where's she going?' Quinn asked.

Nord craned his sinuous neck around. 'Only one act of spite is left to Warathu now. She means to destroy my home.'

CHAPTER 14

STORM DRAGON

Ignus and Ulric charged into the town square from two different directions, each one herding a group of possessed citizens. The mountain spirits screeched and snarled angrily, jabbering curses in forgotten tongues. Ulric breathed short blasts of flame, enough to make the vassals recoil but not to hurt them.

In the midst of the spirits stood Morton, who was trying to rally them. 'Stand fast!' he hissed. 'Tear the dragons apart!'

'Welcome back, Nord! Glad you saw sense in

the end,' roared Ulric as he swatted a mountain spirit out of the sky.

'Get after the doctor,' Ignus urged. 'We've got the situation under control here . . .'

A volley of ice-spears came whistling towards Ignus. With a fiery blast, he melted almost all of them in mid-flight. One spear struck his eye and he went staggering back, half-blind and crying out in pain.

'Doesn't look under control to me,' Thea said. 'Quinn, we have to help them. They're outnumbered.'

'We can't,' Quinn told her. 'We have to stop Warathu, and then the others will fall. Come on!'

'But they're your friends! You can't just leave them!' Thea protested.

Nord's steely voice rang out: 'They may fall today. That was the choice they made. Honour their bravery, Thea. They are giving us a chance, so let us take it!' He flew up and out of the square, heading for the White Tower.

Without a word, Thea climbed on top of

Quinn's back and together they flew over the Citadel rooftops, following Nord.

The sounds of battle echoed from the town square. Quinn forced himself not to look back.

The White Tower loomed before them, stark and silent as an abandoned lighthouse. Quinn could see no trace of Warathu. The dragons circled the tower, looking for some sign of the doctor's presence.

'There!' Nord darted towards the shattered remains of two glass doors. Quinn recognised the balcony where he and Thea had sat only days before. Warathu had broken into the tower from halfway up.

Quinn flew close so that Thea could dismount safely, then he and Nord shifted back to their human forms. There was no doubting which way Warathu had fled. A trail of splintered doors, shattered furniture and patches of sparkling ice marked the spirit's trail.

'She's heading upstairs,' Nord said. 'This way.'

The three of them sprinted up the tower stairs. On the next floor they found De Witt, sprawled motionless. Nord knelt down and cradled the man's head.

De Witt's eyes flickered open. 'Muh . . . my lord? Is that you? I am so sorry. I failed you.'

'Quiet – it's all right.'

'I wasn't strong enough. I couldn't stop her . . .'

'You did well,' Nord said softly. 'Rest now.'

Nord lowered his servant's body to the ground again. There was a terrible look in his eyes. From overhead came a crack and rumble of thunder.

As they climbed the stairs, they found more evidence of Warathu's presence. Portraits of family members lay shredded, their frames broken. A drinking horn, preserved for centuries, had been crushed to fragments. Servants were sprawled unconscious, or sat huddled and shivering from unbearable cold.

At last they reached the library. The doors stood open. The doctor hovered halfway up the hollow tower, with ropy snakes of ice-pale light arcing down from her hands to the floor. She laughed to see Nord enter: 'A gift for you, little lord, from one ruler to another!'

Quinn shoved Nord out of the way just as the doctor loosed a devastating ice-blast more powerful than anything before. A mass of ice the size of a hay bale smashed down through the floorboards. It kept going, with crash after crash echoing up from below as it broke through each floor in turn.

The doctor laughed. 'I will tear your home down around you, Nord. You cannot stop me.'

Nord bared his teeth. In a flash he shifted to dragonform, still snarling. 'Stop you? I will *end* you.'

That just made the spirit laugh all the harder. 'And end the innocent life whose body I have borrowed? Would you really kill one helpless woman, even if it meant saving thousands?'

Nord roared and lashed his tail in frustration.

We can't win this, Quinn thought desperately. *There's no way to destroy Warathu without killing the doctor too! We'd have to purge the spirit from her body somehow . . .*

Wait! PURGE. I've heard that word not long ago. But where?

A sudden thought struck him. He grabbed Thea's arm. 'That spell! Remember you said you knew a spell to purge the body?'

'Yes, it's for when people eat poison berries and . . . oh. OH.' Her eyes widened. 'I see what you mean!'

'Will it work?'

Thea raised her hands. 'It's got to be worth a try . . .'

The doctor set about toppling Nord's bookcases, laughing at the destruction. Thea focused her will, concentrating and chanting. She clenched her fist.

'Wait . . . no! What magic is this?' The doctor wailed and juddered in the air like a puppet, held in the grip of Thea's magic. Black torrents of cloudy matter began to pour from her mouth and eyes. Thea kept up the low murmur of her magical chant.

'It's working!' Quinn yelled. 'She's forcing the spirit out!'

The doctor's body sank down and down as more of Warathu's substance was wrenched from its host. Eventually she collapsed, as limp and loose as an empty sack.

Warathu loomed in the library tower, finally visible in her true form, a bloated, cloudy mass with long spectral tendrils trailing down below. Quinn thought she looked like a monstrous jelly-fish.

Nord opened his jaws, but before he could breathe out, three of the tendrils lashed out. They caught Nord, Thea and Quinn and twined around their bodies, choking the life out of them.

Quinn shifted into dragonform alongside Nord, thinking it would be easier to resist the spirit's deadly embrace if he had a dragon's strength. Thea had no such luck. She let out a scream as Warathu strangled and squeezed her all at once, like a foul serpent crushing the breath out of its prey.

'Nord!' Quinn gasped. 'We have to attack. Now!'

Nord strained, and with a mighty cry he burst free from the crushing grip. Fragments of the spirit's body went flying, torn asunder by the

Storm Dragon's power. Warathu let out a low, booming groan.

'So, you *can* be hurt!' Nord beat his wings and a roaring wind swept through the library tower. Pages fluttered loose and whole volumes went tumbling from the shelves. He beat them harder, his eyes shining bright, and the wind became a hurricane. Warathu was hurled from one side of the tower to the other, still looking like a vast jellyfish, but now she was a jellyfish in raging waters.

Nord was truly the master of the storm and his vengeance was great. The hurricane ripped and tore at Warathu, shredding her. Great hanks of black spirit-stuff came tumbling off her body.

She wailed, her voice growing high and thin, like the sound of a deflating balloon. Nord glared at the dying spirit without mercy.

In moments, there was nothing left of Warathu but a jumbled confusion of ragged scraps dancing about in the whirling chimney of wind. Was that the end of her? Quinn needed to be sure.

He blew a stream of freezing wind over the spectral remains. They became flying boulders of ice, bashing against one another in the vortex. Nord bowed his head; the wind suddenly dropped and for a second there was deafening silence.

Then the frozen fragments fell, shattering on the floor.

Warathu was gone. All that was left of her were little scattered mounds of dirty ice, melting into puddles as Quinn watched.

Thea rubbed her throat, gasping. 'We did it. Holy gods, Quinn. We destroyed her.'

And then they heard a shattering *bang* from several floors below . . .

CHAPTER 15

CATHERINE

Quinn and Thea raced down the spiral stairs after Nord. They ran into the entrance hall, only to see jagged fragments of marble scattered everywhere.

'Catherine's statue!' Thea said in dismay. 'Warathu destroyed it. What a heartless –'

'I don't think that's what happened,' Quinn said. 'Look.' He pointed at a huddled human form that lay in the midst of the debris.

'Impossible!' Nord gasped.

They rushed over to the figure that was struggling to sit up. From her long, tangled black hair, Quinn could already see who it was. It was as if a spirit was being torn from the statue itself . . .

'Catherine?' Nord gasped, tears brimming in in his eyes. 'You're alive!'

Catherine looked stunned and sleepy, like she'd woken from the depths of eternal slumber. She put her hands up to her face to examine them, like she couldn't believe they were real.

'N-Nord,' she stammered, staring down at the broken marble surrounding her. 'What's going on?'

'So this is what happened!' he cried. 'All this time, you were right beside me . . . and I never knew? Warathu must have –'

At the sound of Warathu's name Catherine bristled and looked round frantically. 'Where is she? Nord, we're in great danger –'

Quinn gave a little laugh and stepped in. 'Catherine, I think you have some catching up to do . . .'

That evening, Nord ordered a feast. The White Tower was no longer quiet. It thronged with townsfolk, free from the mountain spirits, eager to show their thanks to their lord and his cohorts. Hundreds of them came to bring presents of food, ale, fruit and fragrant teas, until it seemed the great table must crack under the weight. Quinn lost count of all the backslapping and handshakes the citizens of Auric had given him.

Ignus had been right about Catherine. Quinn *did* like her. He sat beside her in the grand dining hall, along with Thea and the other Dragon Knights, and listened to her tell her story, and filled her in on his. Doctor Margery Devereux sat with them, fully recovered now, and eating as if she had been starved for ten years. Nord held Catherine's hand as if he never meant to let it go again.

'The night Nord left to fight against Vayn, Doctor Devereux and I went to confront Warathu ourselves,' Catherine explained. 'First, I cast half a dozen protective spells, just to be safe. Then we meant to make a bargain with the mountain spirits. If they would leave us alone, we would give them gifts in token of respect. That way, we might have a chance at peace.' She took a swig of ale and smacked her lips with relish. 'Unfortunately, as it turned out, Vayn had already made a deal of his own.'

'I knew Vayn had to be behind this,' said Quinn.

'The doctor and I went out on the Winter Eyrie,' Catherine continued, 'and called on Warathu by name, demanding she speak with us in peace. When the Seraphic Lights appeared in the sky, I thought it was her, but it wasn't. It was Vayn. First, he helped Warathu take over the doctor's body. After that I don't remember a thing. But the pair of them must have combined their magic to imprison me in my own statue.'

Despite the horrible experiences she was describing, Catherine's voice was calm and steady.

'So that was Vayn's plan,' Thea said, sounding almost in awe of it. 'He provided Warathu with a body – poor Doctor Margery's body – in exchange for Warathu's help later on.'

Catherine nodded. 'Warathu wanted revenge

on the people of Auric. Vayn used that as a bargaining chip.'

'He took you away from me,' Nord said, with deep menace in his voice. 'He threatened my people. A thousand deaths will not be enough for that man. And yet . . .'

Catherine raised an eyebrow. 'Yes?'

'If I leave Auric, I risk losing you again.'

Catherine took Nord's hand in both of hers. 'Listen to me, Nord. I love you with all my heart, but if you even think of staying here instead of joining the fight against Vayn, I will skin you alive and wear your hide as a party frock.'

Nord laughed despite himself. 'Even if I become a dragon?'

'Especially then. Your silver scales would look prettier on me, don't you think?'

As Nord blushed and everyone laughed, she turned to Quinn. 'That reminds me. They say you have golden dragon scales. Has anyone told you what they mean?'

'No. Can you?'

Catherine smiled. 'Oh, yes. All those hours in the library were bound to come in useful some day. It's simple: you're a great dragon.'

'That's what Warathu kept calling me!' Quinn exclaimed.

'She was right to. A great dragon is one with elemental power over earth, air, fire and water. They are incredibly rare.'

Quinn sat in stunned silence. Everyone looked at him, thinking their own thoughts. Eventually Thea spoke up:

'So that explains why you can breathe ice as well as fire. You're not an Earth Dragon like your father at all. You're much, much more than that . . .'

Nord cleared his throat. 'My friends, since we are gathered under my roof, I propose one final toast. To the Dragon Knights, and to the future. You will always be welcome in the White Tower.' He raised his glass.

'A final toast?' Quinn said, unsure what Nord meant. 'So what happens next?'

Nord kissed Catherine's hand and looked

Quinn in the eye. 'Your Majesty, tomorrow I say farewell to Auric, for we set out in search of the next Dragon Knight. And together we will put an end to Vayn, once and for all!'

DRAGON KNIGHTS

NORD THE STORM DRAGON

DRAGONFORM

Nord is an icy-blue dragon with piercing eyes, wide wings
and a long, spiky frill.

BACKGROUND

Nord is a serious, noble Dragon Knight. Born of an ancient
family that lived high in the Auric Citadel for generations,
his dragonblood abilities came as a surprise at an early age.
He was drafted into the inner circle of Dragon Knights
when he was young, so even though 12 years have passed
since Vayn took charge, he's more youthful than the likes of
Ignus and Ulric.

OCCUPATION

When he was stripped of his powers, Nord returned to the
Auric Citadel and his family's ancestral home. Finding that
his betrothed had disappeared, Nord was devastated. He

DRAGON KNIGHTS

decided to live a quiet life, isolated from all of Alariss's concerns, including the violence and destruction of Vayn's rule. Nord spends his days practising archery, the citadel's favourite pastime.

ATTRIBUTES

Nord can come across as stern and even arrogant at times, but this is because he desires order, calm and balance.

STRENGTHS

Nord was never a born fighter; instead, he uses his intelligence and strategic thinking to defeat his enemies. However, when he needs to, Nord can unleash devastating force on his foes. As a Storm Dragon he has the power to breathe icy winds over his opponents, freezing them on the spot. He can also whip up brutal hurricanes with his wings.

WEAKNESSES

Nord has a tendency to go it alone and isn't always a strong team player. He is often happiest on his own, and needs reminding that to defeat the strongest foe the Dragon Knights must work together.

Piccadilly
PRESS

Thank you for choosing a Piccadilly Press book.

If you would like to know more about our authors, our books or if you'd just like to know what we're up to, you can find us online.

www.piccadillypress.co.uk

You can also find us on:

We hope to see you soon!